Scholastic Children's Books
An imprint of Scholastic Ltd
Euston House, 24 Eversholt Street, London, NW1 1DB, UK
Registered office: Westfield Road, Southam, Warwickshire, CV47 0RA
SCHOLASTIC and associated logos are trademarks and/or
registered trademarks of Scholastic Inc.

First published in the UK by Scholastic Ltd, 2020

Trade ISBN 978 1 407188 58 4

A CIP catalogue record for this book
is available from the British Library.

Printed by CPI Group (UK) Ltd, Croydon, CR0 4YY
Papers used by Scholastic Children's Books are made
from wood grown in sustainable forests.

1 3 5 7 9 10 8 6 4 2

This is a work of fiction. Names, characters, places, incidents
and dialogues are products of the author's imagination or are used
fictitiously. Any resemblance to actual people, living or dead,
events or locales is entirely coincidental.

www.scholastic.co.uk

Macbeth United

Michael Rosen

Illustrated by
Tony Ross

■ SCHOLASTIC

CHAPTER 1

Elgin Radio

*E*LGIN RADIO, a small local radio station. It's housed in an office block in the centre of town. It was once modern-looking, all glass, steel and bold blue colours, but everything seems to have faded and there are the first signs of neglect: a crack in a ceiling here, a peeling bit of wallpaper there, the odd broken tile on the floor.

Mike Le Rose is one of the main anchormen at the station. He's in his fifties, rather full of himself, thinks he knows everything, and he rather enjoys having a dig at any of the younger people at the station, especially Costas. Costas is the youngest and keenest on Elgin Radio, working long hours, often for free.

Mike: This is me, Mike Le Rose, with you on Elgin Radio. I'm with you here in the studio but looking out at the outside world, the glorious Elgin Radio car park, and I can see it's pretty chilly out there.

One person who'll know all about the weather is our sports correspondent – and the maker of the worst cup of tea in Elgin Radio – Costas.

Costas, dear listeners, is at a very special match between the two top youth teams in the city.

Costas: A chilly day, indeed, Mike! And I'm here without my thermal undies.

Mike: Don't think we need to know that, Costas.

Talk us through the match: this is a Youth Cup final, but today these are very special youth teams, am I right?

Costas: You're always right, Mike. And it is special, because these two teams – like all the other teams in this tournament – are run by the lads themselves. No adult coaches. This is a remarkable—

Mike: Sorry to interrupt, Costas, but let's concentrate on the game. How's it going, what's happening as we approach the end of the match?

Costas: Well, Mike, yes, as you say, we're into the last few minutes and this game really could go either way. Top team, North Road, full of promise and poise. They have had most of the possession, but Shotfield, a team packed with talent, have looked dangerous on the break.

I thought Shotfield were going to miss Duncan, their team captain, player-manager – call it how you like – but not at all.

Mike: Who's caught your eye, Costas?

Costas: Well, there's one lad who has indeed caught my eye: it's Shotfield's striker, Macbeth. He's strong, he puts himself about, and he looks sharp. He gets himself into that little pocket just in front of North Road's central defence and he's been causing them all sorts of problems. Keep an eye on him.

And Andersen for North Road too. He's been the lynchpin for them. Everything good that North Road are doing has come through him. If I was going to put my money on this, this late in the game, I'd say that North Road could grab this at the death. And if they do, it'll be down to Andersen.

Mike: Well, listeners, remember those names.

Costas: I have to say, these lads are showing some older players I know how the game should be played: keeping the ball on the floor, a lot of running off the ball. Players like Macbeth, Banks, Malcolm, Cawdor, Angus – the assistant coach standing in for Duncan today – have all put in a shift, getting into open spaces, offering themselves. It really is "the beautiful game", as the Brazilian great, Pelé, called it...

Mike: Actually, Costas, I think that was another Brazilian player, Didi, but I get your point. Though there are some who—

Costas: GOAL! With so little time left, that must be all over.

Mike: Which way?

Costas: Oh, hang on ... hang on... I thought it was a goal. From where I'm standing, pitch-side, I thought that went in. North Road's goalie was out of position. Cawdor, who's also the assistant coach for today, had three-quarters of the goal to shoot at, and it's gone wide. I saw the net shake, but it's just the side-netting.

Mike: So, no goal?

Costas: Malcolm's waving his arms about. He thinks Cawdor should have passed it to him. That was a big miss. Cawdor should have done better. Or passed it to Malcolm. And Malcolm has been outstanding today.

Mike: Listeners, we'll stay with this youth final. We're getting a lot of texts and tweets asking us to. Here at Elgin Radio we like to respond to what you want. As we say, "If we're not local, we're nothing." So over once again to Costas, for what must be the last minute of the game. And we can only hope that Costas can make sure we know what's going on as it happens, eh, Costas? If it stays nil-nil it'll go straight to penalties, no extra-time, I think.

Costas: I'm doing my best here, Mike. Shotfield have got possession yet again for what must be their last chance. Malcolm has the ball, slips it to Banks. Now North Road's Andersen has gone in on Banks ... that looks a bit high to me, ref says no, waves play on and Andersen's come away with the ball. This could be dangerous. Like I said, everything's come through Andersen. He could be through here. This could be the decider.

What?! Oh no! Goodness me. No!

Mike: Costas? Costas? What? What's going on? Are you still there?

Costas: I'm here. I'm very much here. Sheesh! That was ... that was...

Mike: What?

Costas: I can't put it into words.

Mike: But that's your job, Costas.

Costas: I'm trying. Andersen had the ball on his favoured left foot. He's through on goal and is just about to hit the ball across, into the top corner, when Macbeth's come in from the side, but just as he's come flying in, Andersen has pulled his elbow back right into Macbeth's face... Macbeth's carried on into Andersen – it's a flying tackle really... He's got the ball all right ... goal-saving tackle, no question, but he's ended up high on Andersen's standing leg and Andersen's gone down like a log.

Mike: So is it a red card for Macbeth? What's going on?

Costas: No! I can't believe I'm saying this.

Macbeth's not off. Andersen's down. I don't know if the ref's missed it or whether he thinks it was fifty-fifty. Or perhaps he thinks it was fine because Macbeth's got the ball. Another ref might have sent them both off. Double red. Double yellow at the very least.

Mike: Is Andersen injured?

Costas: Blood's streaming down his leg. He can't go on playing. North Road's coach is on the field. He's taking Andersen off! That's their number sixteen getting ready to come on for the dying seconds. Oh no!

Mike: You're breaking up, Costas. What's going on now?

Costas: Hey, that's bad. That's really bad. I saw that. As Macbeth walks back towards the rest of the Shotfield team, he's winked. I saw it quite clearly, he's winked. He knows what he's doing there. He's taken Andersen out of the game. There's going to be afters, Mike. But hey, the ref looks like he's changed his mind: he has given them both a yellow card. Quite right.

Mike: Maybe the wink just meant that he was OK.

Costas: I don't think so. And that's a high five. Shotfield are making out that Macbeth's some kind of hero.

Mike: You did say it was a goal-saving tackle, Bill. How much more on the clock?

Costas: Three minutes. Stay with me, Mike, if you can. Don't go to the shopping news just yet. There has to be a result here.

Mike: Will do.

Costas: North Road with the ball now, slipping it around at the back quite slickly. Maybe they're playing for penalties. A neat pass forward to their sub, number sixteen — oh, careless, he's lost it. Andersen would have done better there.

So it's with Shotfield now, Malcolm to Banks, lovely cross-ball left to right to Macbeth, back to Banks who's broken down that left side. Back into the centre with Malcolm, just in the spot where Andersen was tackling back earlier. Maybe Andersen would have taken the ball off Malcolm there.

For people just joining us: no Andersen on now. Off injured.

Malcolm is on his own, beats one, beats two,

edge of the area – he can't shoot from there, surely. HE HAS! HE HAS! HE HAS! It's in!

That. Is. A wondergoal.

Mike: Amazing!

Costas: That could have graced any pitch anywhere in the world. It's started off outside the right-hand post and it's curled and it's curled and it's curled in, just under the bar, and inside the upright. Top right-hand corner. Postage stamp. By airmail. Express delivery. Don't return to sender.

Huge celebrations for Shotfield. They think they've won this.

Mike: Amazing stuff, Costas. Stay with us, listeners. We'll have the shopping news for you in just a moment.

Costas: North Road want to start it again quickly. We're well into added time now.

Ref blows for the restart. North Road are taking it down the right... It's into the centre.

Are they going to snatch a draw?

Surely not.

Dramatic scenes here. The sub has got it. The North Road bench are screaming at him. It's the lad who's come on for Andersen. He's going to shoot. No. He dummies. Shotfield's goalie, Rossi, has slipped. It's fooled him. Open goal. This must be a goal.

And ... he's put it OVER!!!

The sub has put it over. Sorry, I don't know his name. He's missed. It was their chance.

Rossi has gone behind the goal to retrieve the ball and ... that's the whistle. The ref's blown.

It's over. Shotfield have won! Shotfield have won!

I thought North Road were going to even it up at the death. Shotfield were careless. It could easily have gone to penalties. I can't help thinking that if Andersen had still been on, it would have been penalties. But the sub has muffed it. Poor lad. He's in tears. He knows what could have been.

Back to you in the studio, Mike.

Mike: Thank you, Costas. Fantastic scenes, then, there at Bittle Stadium. A game that could have gone either way. Fantastic goal from Malcolm. And Macbeth – hero or villain, Costas? What do you think?

Costas: That's anyone's call at this stage, Mike. I'm sure that tackle will be talked about for a long time to come. Macbeth's tackle sure was a game-changer.

Mike: Game-changer indeed. Thanks very much, Costas. We'll be back at the Bittle Stadium to hear from managers and players in just a moment. But right now, it's the shopping news.

CHAPTER 2

Duncan

"**D**uncan! For goodness' sake, put your blooming phone down and come over here. Your nanna's brother wants to meet you. He's come all the way from Spain for this."

It was the wedding that spoiled everything. The dream-breaker.

Duncan looked at his mother. She was loving it. Rushing about between guests, in her brand-new pink dress, rings, necklace, bracelets gleaming.

Why, why, why did it have to be on the day of

the Youth Cup final? Wasn't Shotfield *Duncan's* team? *We are one of the best teams out of all the youth-run teams in the area, aren't we?* And was he the player-coach, or not? Was he one of the best, or not? *Come on!* Wasn't he THE best player? Well, now – from what he was picking up on his phone – it was sounding like Macbeth was today's hero…

"Duncan! I don't want to have to tell you again!"

He had just heard Shotfield had won. Good news or bad news? Well, yes, of course it was good news. It was great news. But there was just a little bitsy teeny bit of him that was miffed. He should have been there. He should have been a part of it. He should have been the one having the cup handed to him. Yeah, yeah, now the pics were coming through from his mates:

Us with the cup!

Malcolm with the cup!

Mack with the cup!

The cup, the cup, the cup!

Oh, there was a nice text:

All down to you, Dunk! You trained us, bro!

Nice one, Mack. That made him feel a bit better.

He put his ear to the phone again. He didn't want to disrupt this wedding any more than he had to. He could hear the players talking to that crazy Elgin Radio guy, Mike Le Rose. He was going on and on and on about that tackle.

His mother's voice drifted into his ears again: "Duncan. I'm not asking, I'm telling. Come and meet your nanna's brother, Federico. You remember I've always told you there's football in our blood. Well, this is what I meant. When he was a lad, he played for Real Madrid."

"What?" said Duncan. "Really? Did he?"

Finally, his mother had got his attention. "He might have done," she said with a smile.

"OK, you win. I was just catching up on the team."

"I'm sorry, Dunko, I know you are."

"You didn't think we'd play well enough

in the earlier rounds to make it all the way to the final, did you?" said Duncan sadly. "We won and I had to miss it, all because of this stupid wedding. I told you that this wedding clashed with the day of the final."

Duncan's mum ruffled his hair. He pulled himself away. The hall was full, the speeches were over, and the lights were dimming. It would be the disco in a minute. Duncan looked across at all the people. Some he didn't know at all. Some were faces he knew from old photos. Some were people he knew only too well. People sat in clusters and pairs, old heads nodding and smiling. Young people standing about in new clothes that were too big or old ones that were too small. The beams from the lights sprayed out across the room in a dizzy display.

"Did you hear me, Mum? We won."

"Well, that's good news," she said. Duncan looked at her. He would have preferred it if she had said that it was a pity that he hadn't been there to have won it. Wasn't it *his* team, he heard himself think again?

"Now come on and meet Federico," she added, "and you can find out who he did play for. What's that other Spanish team called...?"

"Costa Brava," he said, as he got up and headed off with his mother across the dance floor.

"That's the one," she said.

"No, Mum," he laughed, "Costa Brava isn't a football team! It's where all the resorts are."

His mother ignored him, nodded and smiled at the guests, hugged an old man whose chicken-loaded fork was mid-air. She shrieked and giggled with two teenage girls with the biggest eyelashes that he had ever seen. This walk across the room was turning into an epic journey.

Then his phone buzzed. It was a text. From Rossi:

Hi, Dunk. Great we did it, huh? V sorry u not here. For real. Weird stuff going down. Big bust-up between Malcolm and Cawd. Cawd says everyone down on him. Says he might go for trials with Angles. Then Malcolm says Cawd missed that shot on purpose. Cawd went for him. Landed one on him. Mack pulled him off and told him to clear off. Not gd.

While Mum carried on hugging, Duncan stood in the middle of the room fuming.

Cawd's blown it. I've had enough. He's finished. Maybe I'll make Mack assistant coach. I'll give

Rossi a call later and talk it over with him...

He texted back:

`Thnx Rossi.`

Then there was Mum in his ear again: "I told you to put that phone down and come and meet your great-uncle Federico. He played for Juventus."

"Juventus is an Italian team."

"What are you saying? Just because he's Spanish, he can't play for an Italian side? Now come on and meet the great man. You must have inherited all that great football talent you tell me about from him... Federico! *Hola*, Federico! *Aquí está el niño. También es un gran futbolista...*"

CHAPTER 3

Macbeth

*I*t was getting dark.

It was late in the day; Macbeth and Banksy were crossing Heathstead Common, on the way to meeting up with Duncan for Thursday night training.

The lights from the street lamps on the edge of the common looked like white moons hanging in the night sky, a great black dome over their heads. There was something unreal about it, as if they were figures in a painting, and their breath puffed out in front of them for just a second before vanishing for ever. But vanishing where? Macbeth could still feel Andersen's elbow-jab on the side of his face ... and if he was honest with himself, he could also feel on his foot where he had gone in on Andersen in the tackle that took him off. And as Macbeth thought that, the picture of the blood on Andersen's leg flared up behind his eyes. Red and sticky, the brightest thing on that cold, dull day of the match.

But, hey, I'm a player, he thought. *The big games are about getting the tiny things right – "small margins", as they say on TV. If I'd missed the ball, I would have been off. Deffo. A split-second difference – I would have been the villain and we would have lost it. Instead, I'm the hero.* He loved thinking of that word: hero. *That's me. Hero.*

"Do you ever get spooked by this place?" Banksy asked, pacing along beside him.

A mist sat low over the darkening grass.

For a second Macbeth had forgotten that Banksy was with him. *Good old Banksy.* Not tall, not short. Solid. Square.

"Nah!" said Macbeth, pulling his chin in and narrowing his eyes, "as if!" He knew that it came out too quick and too loud to be convincing: no one liked being out on Heathstead Common in the night, but the alternative was to walk all round the edge. *No thanks.*

Then the blood-picture came back to him: Andersen's leg. For a moment, he felt bad about it. Then he felt the elbow in his face again. *It could have been me. If Andersen's arm had been two centimetres higher it could have bust my eye, like an MMA fighter's.* Didn't Duncan say that he, Macbeth, would be good at mixed martial arts? *Yes, I would,* he thought. In a way, that tackle was an MMA moment. And that thought made him feel in his body that things were never going to be quite the same. He glanced at Banksy walking along beside him. *Yes, he is good guy, Banksy, but has he got that extra thing, that thing that takes you to the next level?*

They walked on and on across the painting, and for a moment it felt that no matter how fast they walked they got no nearer to the moons.

Into his mind came the sound of a cough. Where from? It felt like it came from behind.

They both glanced round together. About twenty metres back, standing in the low-hanging mist, were three guys. Grown men. They had grown up out of the ground like three dark trees and now stood in midst of the mist. Macbeth and Banksy turned to face them. They both felt their hearts beat anxiously. The men's faces seemed to blur into their bulky coats, and they were too far off for their eyes to show, so they were faceless. Macbeth moved his shoulders, ready to walk on.

"Well done, lads," said one.

"Yes, well done," said the other in a strange, echoey way.

"Good job," said the third.

The three men stayed put, twenty metres off. Something about them gave the boys a reason to stay put too. Macbeth wondered if he could get away from these guys if it came to a chase.

"We were there," said one.

"You played well," said the other.

"Good work," said the third.

Banksy came back at them: "You saw the game?"

"Uh-huh," said one.

"Of course," said the other.

"Guys like us never miss a Youth Cup final," said the third.

"Who are you?" said Macbeth.

"Oh, nothing much," said one.

"You could say we're lookouts," said the other.

"Always on the lookout," said the third.

"You're the assistant coach for the team, aren't you?" said the first to Macbeth.

"No," Macbeth replied, "that's Cawdor. I'm Macbeth."

"Cawdor, Macbeth. Macbeth, Cawdor," said the other in a sing-song voice and shrugged, as if there really wasn't any difference between them.

"Do you want to be a footballer? I mean, a real footballer," said the second one to Macbeth.

"Well, yeah... I kind of am."

"No, no, no," said the third, "to be a footballer, you've got to get yourself into an academy."

"And," said one, "to get into an academy, to get noticed, you've got to show real knowledge of the game. Teamwork knowledge and leadership. It's not just about skill."

"Look, who are you?" It was Banksy this time.

"We're, like … scouts."

"Scouting around, looking for real players. Not flashy, fly-by-night players. Ones that'll stay the course."

"You, lad," said the second to Banksy, "you're good. You're very good."

"You, lad," said the third to Macbeth, "you're good, but you need to push yourself on. Now that you're assistant coach, you—"

"I'm not assistant coach," interrupted Macbeth.

The man went on as if Macbeth hadn't spoken: "You should be thinking of becoming head coach. You could do it. Leadership on and off the pitch. That's what they're looking for."

"Who?" Macbeth asked. The question slipped into the mist. There was no reply.

Banksy shifted from one foot to the other. The

noise of his feet seemed to draw the men's attention back to him.

One of them picked up the cue. "You're a bit younger than him, aren't you?"

"Uh-huh," Banksy said, not wanting to admit it.

"One day, you're going to make it, too. We see you boys come and go. We get to be nigh on one-hundred-per-cent accurate about which ones will make it. We can see it in you, even when you're younger. The spark we're looking for... One day that'll be a real fire in you."

"You've got the spark. Just like Cawdor here. He's got the fire."

"I'm not Cawdor," said Macbeth, quite angrily this time. "Come on, Banksy, let's go. We'll be late." And even as he said that, that seemed to push the three men back into the dark mist as quickly as they first appeared.

It was over.

"Hey, that was seriously weird, Mack," said Banksy. "Seriously wee-eirrddd."

Banksy had said what Macbeth was thinking.

"Yeah," he agreed, "it was." And he meant it.

They walked on across the common towards the moons. Now they were getting nearer. The hum of traffic grew in their ears, and there was no mist here. *Shy of the cars purring past?* Macbeth wondered.

"Why did he keep calling you Cawdor, like he thought you ... you were, you know, assistant coach, or something?" Banksy asked.

"Dunno," said Macbeth, keeping himself locked in. He noticed something about the way Banksy had asked him that. It was as if Banksy was seeing things falling into some sort of order. Was the thinking how one day Macbeth was going to be head coach and next he would be?

Macbeth looked at him: younger, smaller, always neat, tidy, always passed the ball straight to the man.

Hmmm, he probably thinks that all he has to do is be patient, Macbeth thought. *Mr Reliable Banksy probably thinks how all he needs to do is take his turn, his time will come. I'm more of a dive-in, do-it, see-what-happens guy, aren't I?* Then straight away after, he wondered if he really was that guy.

As they got near to the road and the light, they both started to relax. They caught up with Rossi and Angus.

"Hey!"

"Hey!" Macbeth didn't want to say anything about the three weird guys on the common and hoped that Banksy wouldn't say anything either.

"You OK?" said Angus, looking at him rather closely.

"Sure," said Macbeth, "why do you ask?"

"I dunno. You look kinda twitchy."

"Do I?"

"No," said Angus, rolling his eyes, "That's why I didn't ask!"

"And well done today," said Rossi.

"Hey, look, you've done that already," said

Macbeth. "Cheers all the same, but it was all of us. Really. We're a team, right?" He held out his fist for a little fist-touch.

"No, I meant the other thing…"

"What other thing?"

Rossi looked from one to the other and back again.

"You didn't … er…?"

"I don't know what you're talking about," Macbeth said, a little more snappily than he intended.

"I mean," said Rossi, talking like he thought it was obvious, "well done on becoming assistant."

Macbeth felt himself gasp silently. And was that a gasp from Banksy at the same time?

"I'm … er … assistant?" he asked. "Assistant? How come? I mean, how do you know?"

"Oh, sorry, I thought Dunk told you. You should probably check your phone; Dunk's been calling people. He heard about Cawd missing that shot, and the bust-up with Malcolm. And then, you know Cawd's been gabbing on about he was going to a trial with Angles, so…" Rossi shrugged and did his favourite gesture: tapping one hand under the other as if he was flicking a ball out of the room.

Angus chipped in: "I think he missed that shot on purpose."

"Never!" said Rossi, who liked things to be straight because he was a straight-up sort of guy himself. Or at least wanted everyone to think he was.

"Are you saying that I am, you know, assistant now?"

"Sure."

"Wow!" Mack said. "Wow!" he said again.

"Don't get overheated, Mack," Rossi said, a little taken aback by Mack's reaction. "I don't think Dunk's told Cawd yet. But he will."

Macbeth could feel
that he had suddenly
become out of breath. He
glanced over at Banksy,
who was staring at him.
Their eyes met. They each

looked into each other's minds and saw the same
thing: the three shapes back there in the mist on
the common telling them things. Telling them things
that both made sense and didn't make sense.

Macbeth was assistant coach. He had replaced
Cawdor. He had become Cawdor.

But ... but ... how did those three shapes know
that ... like, before it happened?

CHAPTER 4

Duncan

*D*uncan, Malcolm and Cawdor were doing their stretches. Duncan leaned on Malcolm's shoulder and pulled his foot up behind him, stretching his quads.

"...and seven and eight and nine and ten," he breathed into the air.

He swapped legs.

"And one and two and three and..."

Cawdor was on the ground flattening his legs against the all-weather pitch and curling up his toes. "I'm sorry. Look, I'm saying it: I'm sorry," he muttered.

Duncan and Malcolm ignored him.

"I was... Look, anyone could have... I mean, I bet you've done stuff not thinking it through."

He's whingeing, Duncan thought, and he and Malcolm went on ignoring him. Duncan went on pumping out the reps:

"...and seven and eight and nine..."

Now Cawdor was more accusing. "You told him, didn't you?" he said to Malcolm.

"Sure I did," Malcolm clipped back, "and if you don't know why I told him, then you're not getting it."

"Getting what?"

"You're not getting what this is all about," Malcolm grunted to him as he stretched down to the ground. *Good stretching there, Malcolm,* Duncan thought.

Cawdor waited.

Nothing came.

"Go on," Cawdor said in a weak voice.

"It's the team. It's one hundred per cent. You can't be a bit one hundred per cent, or nearly one hundred per cent, or kinda one hundred per cent," Malcolm said, and held the stretch at the very limit.

Cawdor turned to Duncan, who was lifting his legs and swinging them sideways. "Come on, Dunks. You don't have to be like this. I said I was sorry about the thing with Malcolm. And OK, I rang that guy at Angles. I haven't been down there. I just called him. I haven't done the trial. I haven't been there."

"Well, now you can," Duncan said.

"What?" said Cawdor.

"Do the trial," Duncan rapped back sharply.

"I don't get it…" Cawdor looked bothered.

"You're out. You do what you want, now."

"But…"

"Look, Cawd," Duncan said firmly, "it's like we say, at the start of every game: 'Are you in?' And we all shout as loud as we can, 'YOU BET WE'RE IN!!!' That doesn't mean, 'I'm in but I'm going for a trial somewhere else'. So you're out, and you can do what you want now."

Cawdor's face fell. It was clear there was no way back. He turned and walked over to the fence where he had dumped his bag. He picked the bag up, slung it over his shoulder and shambled off out of the gate and out of sight.

Just then Mack, Banksy, Rossi and Angus strolled on to the pitch.

Macbeth

Duncan was on to his over-the-head arm-stretches now. "Hey, Mack," he said, "if you haven't got it from me before, from what the others have said, that was great what you did."

Macbeth felt a rush of thanks flow through him. It felt so good that Dunk was saying this.

But he faked being cool with it: "It was just … just a thing, y'know. I mean, Malcolm's shot … amazing," he said.

"No, no." Duncan wheezed through the next stretch. "That Andersen was bother. I've heard: if he had been on for that last couple of minutes, it could have gone the other way. It was a tipping point. Every game's got a tipping point."

"Well…" Macbeth let his voice fade.

"Anyway, there's something I want to tell you: I'm making you assistant."

"That's great, Dunk, that's great," Macbeth said, partly to Duncan and partly to himself, as that image of the three guys in the dark on the common came up before his eyes ... calling him Cawdor like he was already the assistant before Dunk had even thought of it. *Was that even possible?*

Duncan was still talking: "...and you all know my parents have been talking about moving next year, so I may not be around. So, I know it's not all down to me, but I think if that happens Malcolm should take over. No disrespect to anyone, but I think Malcolm should do the job. It's a leader thing."

"Wow!" Malcolm said. "Wow!" he said again. Duncan had finished his stretches. He didn't have to tell the others to get on with theirs. He paced around, geeing them up: "Right, these games are piling up, 'cos we got so far in the cup. Remember we're at Enver Moss tomorrow? That still OK with everyone? Show of hands."

Duncan raised his own hand. So did everyone else.

"Great. OK, let's do it. Come on!" and Duncan chased off to start doing the "intervals" – sprint and walk, sprint and walk.

Macbeth stared at a worn patch on the pitch.

He felt like he was on the edge of something big, but for the time being he didn't know what, and as he dwelled on the vagueness of that, the picture of the three shapes in the low, dark mist came to him one more time. For a brief moment, he saw them as if they were like the fishermen he'd see on Sundays by the side of the canal, near to his house, and they were all holding the same rod, and he, Macbeth, he could see himself as if he were a fish in the water on the end of their line, being lifted and dropped, lifted and dropped...

"C'mon, guys." Duncan's voice pierced the thought.

And Macbeth joined in, sprint and walk, sprint and walk: the intervals routine. The one that kills.

CHAPTER 5

Mrs Macbeth

"What? On the common? Did you recognize them? Yes, it does sound weird. Very."

Macbeth's mum was laying the table with the phone tucked under her chin. Brisk as ever in her jeans and jumper, everything under control apart from the occasional flick of her right eyelid.

"Hang on – you're sounding muddled – you're telling me that they knew that Dunk would make you assistant before he did? Really?"

She swapped the phone to the other ear and looked out the window.

"Yes, I'm still here; I'm thinking about it, Macky. Things like that make me wonder about stuff. You know how I say that everything happens for a reason? Well, there's a reason here. I can see it. I've told you: it's like a ladder. You're on a ladder. Listen to me, don't ring off. The thing about a ladder is that it doesn't do the climbing for you. You have to do it. You're telling me you're 'assistant coach'. Assistant coach is OK, but now you should be looking up to the next step, *head* coach."

Mack came back at her: "No, Mum, Dunk's already said that Malcolm's going to be the next head coach. Don't start getting ideas."

She had stopped laying the table halfway through, and stood there with one of the knives in her hand.

"What? But weren't you just telling me that these men said that one day you could be? This all fits, Macky. It all fits."

"But—" Mack tried to get a word in.

Mrs Mack wasn't having it.

"No, you listen to me. Never mind what anyone else might think – this is about you. You're being too nicey-nicey. Think it through. These men say that you would be assistant and it turns out they were right. They also say that one day you would be head coach… What does that tell you? Macky, I'm talking to you: what does that tell you?"

Her voice got louder and higher and that right eye twitched. She was prodding the air with the knife as she spoke.

"Look, boy, sometimes things happen to us, sometimes we ourselves make things happen. If a person is too nicey-nicey, they end up being the kind that gets pushed around. I don't want to think that's the kind of person you are. You're going to have to take the next step up that ladder."

She laid the knife on the table and went to fetch the sauces, the phone still stuck under her chin. She heard Mack out for a few seconds and interrupted him again with:

"Stay?! Coming to stay? Who? I mean which of the team want to stay? OK, that's fine. And Dunk! And Dunk? Really? Heavens!"

The salad cream bottle squeezed out of her hand and slid on to the floor.

"That's … that's … no, I just dropped something. Look, I was just laying up for me and you but now the team's coming over, I'll lay out more… See you in a bit. You must be nearly here by now."

She put the phone down and stood there breathing.

She knew herself well enough to recognize these

moments. Ever since he was a baby, she had wanted something special for Macky. It was that feeling that drove her on. Every step he had taken up that ladder, had made that day, that week, that month worth it for her.

She looked down at her hands. She had clenched them till the knuckles had gone white. It was such a fierce thing to do, she thought, it almost scared her. There were things about her health (or was it her mind, she wondered?) that were worrying, and she was always looking for signs that would tell her what was really wrong with her. And, if for a moment she could admit it, she worried that these "moments" she had were something that she might have passed on to Macky.

She looked out the window and stood there for longer than she knew, when the doorbell rang.

It woke her out of her thoughts, and she went to the door: it was the team.

"Thank you very much for letting us stay, Mrs Macbeth," Dunk said in a kind and polite way. The others muttered their thanks along with him. Dunk signed to them to take their shoes off, and as he rose up from putting his pair carefully side-by-side, next to the door, he caught sight of a picture on the wall of a castle.

"Hey, wow! Nice castle," he said.

"Yeah," chipped in Banksy, "my dad took me to one a couple of months ago. The wind at the top was fantastic." He pointed to the battlements on the castle. "It was like that one."

"Yeah," Dunk agreed.

"Glad you like it," said Mrs Macbeth to Dunk in particular. "I always think that if you choose a picture right, it can make a home feel right."

Dunk nodded and smiled.

Mrs Macbeth smiled back.

CHAPTER 6

Macbeth

*M*acbeth slipped up to his room. He was feeling jumpy; everything that had happened over the day was whirling past him down a corridor. The tackle on Andersen, the blood on the leg, the joyful roar of the win, the three men on the common in the dark looming up behind them, their weird Cawdor muddle, and now all these things that Mum was saying...

He looked in the mirror. Was he the kind of person Mum said he had to be?

"Yes," he said to himself: "I am. I am a hero. Now I've got to show it. I'll make a move. Dunk's no better than me. Didn't one of those men say that if I want to be a real footballer, get into an academy, get noticed, get on and up, then I've got to show I know the game? What better way than being a coach? Right. Think of something. Do something, Mack! Tonight, right here, would be a perfect time."

He looked right into his eyes. There was doubt there.

"What am I saying? I can't do something that would bring Dunk down. I've known him since I was a little kid, like he was my cousin, or something. He's great. And anyway, whatever I might do, it would only be found out, and, next thing, they'd be blabbing about it all over the place."

He rammed his hands into his pockets as if to stop them doing anything wrong or bad.

"But how do I climb that ladder that Mum was going on about?"

The moment he thought of Mum, the door

opened and she was right there. It was almost as if he had conjured her up himself.

"Look, Mum, I know what you think: you think I've got to do something to be head coach right now. I know you do – no, don't interrupt – let me finish. But what? I mean, he's just made me assistant, for goodness' sake. What am I supposed to do?"

Mum looked at him. "Just ... be ... brave." She punched the words out one by one. It sounded to Macbeth like she was almost in despair. Pleading with him. He felt himself bending under her weight as he went on looking in the mirror.

She spoke firmly, walking to and fro across Macbeth's room as if there were tracks: "I've had an idea. Why did Cawd get kicked out?" Her eye twitched.

"He was sneaking off to Angles. And he thumped Malcolm, 'cos Malcolm said—"

"Never mind what Malcolm said. So the worst thing any of you can do, is do something – anything – against the team. Am I right?"

"Yep."

Mum left the tracks and slipped to the door to make sure no one was outside. She looked back at him. "So what if … what if … it was found out that Duncan had done something like that as well?" Mum was breathing fire now.

"Like what?"

"Like he had been sending texts to Angles as well … maybe?"

"Well, he hasn't."

"I'm not saying he has," Mum said, no longer pacing to and fro. She had an urgent look in her eyes. "I'm thinking of how he *could* have, if …

someone put some texts on his phone."

"Forget it. That won't work." Even as he said it, Macbeth could see that perhaps it might.

"You're still stuck thinking of what you don't *dare* do. You know very well it *could* work."

"But what if it doesn't?"

"How do you see yourself, Macky? A scaredy-cat? Someone who goes through life talking about all the things he might have done, or could have done, or would have done – but didn't do, because they were things that he didn't *dare* do? You're a great player. But it's not only about that. It's about being at the top so you get noticed. That means getting into an academy, or not."

That hurt. "Don't go there, Mum! I'm..." He hesitated. "I'm doing fine. Just drop it."

There was a lull in the argument. Mrs Macbeth held herself and smoothed down imaginary creases in the arms of her jumper.

This seemed to wind her up to have one more go.

"I can drop it. Of course I can. But let me ask you one thing, Macky: who was it who just told me all that stuff about the three men on the common?"

Macbeth nodded as a way of admitting it was him.

"When you were telling me, I could hear in your voice that you were up for anything, weren't you?"

She was right. That's what being a hero was about. Being up for anything.

She imitated him: "Oh, Mum, I'm assistant now. And they say I'm gonna be the head coach. Yeah, and I'm gonna do what it takes, I—"

It was nasty and it dug into him. He had that bending feeling, as if he were being forced to bend under the pressure.

"All right, all right. I'll ... get my act together and do it."

With just the tiniest of movements at the corners of her mouth – too small to be a smile, but the hint of one even so – Mum turned and went out the room, the right eye firm, not a twitch in sight.

CHAPTER 7

Macbeth

*T*he team lay on the floors of the different rooms as if they had been dumped there for the night. Macbeth could hear them breathing. He could feel their heat fill the rooms. He lay for a while thinking of the night sitting on top of him. It felt like it was trying to squeeze the breath out of him.

He had a sudden urge to go outside and gulp down some fresh air. He stirred, and as he stirred, he heard the groan of one of the others. *Was that*

Dunk? He hoped not, and slipped out the back door into the garden.

The moment he arrived, he heard a voice close by say in a panicky way, "Who's that?"

He recognized Banksy's voice.

"Just me," Macbeth answered.

"Hey, what's the matter? You can't sleep?" Banksy said, almost as if he were accusing Macbeth of something.

"Stuffy in there," he replied.

"I had a weird dream," Banksy said. "Those three guys on the common."

"Them?" Macbeth said in a throwaway fashion. "I'd forgotten about them."

"Forgotten?" Banksy sounded amazed. "What about that thing about how they called you Cawdor, like they *knew* he was going to get chucked off the team and you were going to take over? How did they know?"

"Don't ask me," answered Macbeth, feeling that Banksy was accusing him of having rigged it. "Maybe some other time, y'know, we can talk about it?"

"Mmm, yeah, maybe," Banksy said vaguely into the night air.

Macbeth pulled a leaf off a little apple tree by his side and let it flutter to the ground.

Banksy watched it fall. "Maybe not," he added, and started to move back into the house.

"Hope you sleep OK now," Macbeth said to him, wondering why Banksy seemed less friendly than usual. Was Banksy suspicious that he, his old friend, Mack, was up to something?

"Yep," Banksy said, "and you." And he disappeared into the house. Even the "and you" sounded cold.

Macbeth pulled another leaf off the tree and his eyes followed it to the ground. He looked round, rummaged in his pocket, pulled out a phone, and stared at it. *Was that me who nicked it out of Dunk's jacket earlier? Was that really me? Is this really Dunk's phone?*

The air out in the garden was heavy too. Not enough of a breath even to move the leaves.

He went running on down his tunnel of thoughts: *And if some texts started firing off from this phone, would that really be me sending them, or would it be the phone doing it?*

He shut his eyes and let his mind remember Dunk's password – he'd seen Dunk punch it in once when they were sitting next to each other in the back of Mum's car. Now for the other number: Angles. He held the big number in his head by splitting it into pairs of numbers. He tapped them in at the top of the messages page. Then with his thumb, he wrote:

Hi, Duncan here frm Shotfield. Thnk I'm thru with this lot. Done what I cn with thm. They goin nowhere. frwrds for trial. Cn we talk asap? Duncan.

Macbeth hesitated. He was just about to delete it when he saw Mum's face as it was in his room, talking about the "ladder" and teasing him about what he didn't dare to do.

Well, he said to himself, *I do dare,* and he pressed down hard on *send*.

CHAPTER 8

Macbeth

Macbeth eased the back-door handle down, gently pulled the door open, stepped as lightly as he could on to the mat and pulled the door behind him. He held the door handle down so that there would be no click of the lock, and then, once the door was shut, gently let the handle rise to lock the door.

He let out the smallest of sighs – a sigh of satisfaction, the deed was done. He took a step into the dark of the kitchen, when he felt a hand grip his arm.

He half-expected it to be one of the three men from the common, but it was Mum.

There was a cough. And then another. Someone groaned. Macbeth stared into the dark, afraid that some or all of them would wake up and he would be caught with the phone on him. Neither of them moved.

Mum signed to Macbeth to take the phone and leave it lying on the floor amongst the sleeping team.

The sheer thought of it made Macbeth freeze. A picture appeared in his mind's eye: it was himself bending over with the phone in his hand, and someone – anyone – waking up and sitting bolt upright and grabbing the phone off him. He shut his eyes, but the picture was still there. He opened them again and shook his head. This was a final step he couldn't take.

Mum signed again – faster and more urgently.

Macbeth shook his head again.

Mum gestured disappointment and disgust at him.

She grabbed the phone out of his hand, and another picture came to him, of that time she had wanted him to play the violin in the school orchestra – all that stuff to do with how he was going to be a great musician – and once she was so fed up that he was no good at it, she had grabbed the violin out of his hand and stuffed it in the bin... All that disappointment and disgust sealed up in the gesture. Both times.

She vanished.

Now, there was no way back. A chain of events was about to roll out, a chain that could pull him to the top, just as he and Mum wanted. Or would it be a chain that would wind around him, locking him up tight?

It could go either way.

CHAPTER 9

Macbeth

*M*acbeth was looking through the odd little round window in his bedroom that the builder of the house had put in. He had got some weird idea that it looked a bit boat-like, a bit like a porthole. Macbeth could see the first morning streaks of light. It seemed as if he had been awake all night, churning over and over what he had done, what might happen, what was likely to happen. Or had he sailed through it, dreaming it all? Sometimes the pictures of what he dreamed up merged with the pictures of real things in his memory, and sometimes the whole lot merged with what was going on right in front of him. And what the heck was going to happen? Something in the back of his mind from a science lesson brought the word "chaos" into his mind … drifting towards chaos … chaos, the slow, steady, inevitable slide towards disorder… He started to doze off again, as the word "chaos" slipped across his mind.

There was a loud knocking at the front door.

He got up, but just as he was about to head downstairs and answer it, he heard the sound of Fred coming from outside the house, just outside the front door. Old Fred was the odd-job man, who worked up and down the street clipping hedges, repairing toilets, cleaning cars, clearing gutters. At any moment, Angles could text Dunk and wake them all up. The wait was getting to Macbeth, so he nipped to the loo – but even from the loo he could hear Fred still outside, talking to someone by the front door. He was asking him – or was it them? – who they were.

Then Macbeth heard Duffy and Lennox's voices outside.

"We're in the team. With Mack."

"They should be ready."

"We've got a match."

Ready? Ready?! thought Macbeth, upstairs in the loo. *Oh no! Everyone's still asleep. Wow! What's the time?*

And then back came Fred into his ears: "Well I could let youse in, 'cos I've got a key. I've got keys to most of the houses down here... But I don't know yer, see?"

Macbeth heard the knocking on the front door again.

"Knock, knock, knock," said Fred. "Well, I don't suppose you'd be burglars standing there, a couple of boys in their football kit, and come to think of it, I do recognize you," he added. "Now which key is it? I got so many, see?" He burst into singing one of his old songs, and the raw sound cut into Macbeth's thoughts:

> *"I've got the key of the door,*
> *Never been twenty-one before.*
> *And pa says I can do as I like..."*

He slid from singing the words into whistling the tune as he shook the keys trying to find the right one.

The jangling seemed to shake Macbeth's mind. He knew that bunch of keys very well.

"This one?" said Fred, "Ah no, that must be twenty-nine. Every key's a key to something, eh?"

There was a knock on the door again.

"I said, hold your horses, lads, I'll have it for you in a tick."

Then Macbeth heard Duffy and Lennox talking at Fred in a big hurry, both at the same time. They were saying that they were late. Everyone was late. They had a match to get to.

"Ah well, there you go, lads. I always say, the first hour of the day is worth waiting for: miss that and you miss the best... And you know what that means: "miss the best, miss the rest". Now where have I put that darned key? I've got one of them illegible pens I mark 'em with."

Macbeth hurriedly finished up in the loo, pounded down the stairs, reached the door and opened it, and there stood Duffy, Lennox and old Fred, who was still juggling with his huge bunch of keys.

"Do you know what the time is?"

"We're gonna be late now."

"You've overslept."

"You're still in your pie-jams."

The words came tumbling out of Duffy and Lennox all at the same time. *Never mind the "lull before the storm", as Mum says, this feels like the storm before the storm,* Macbeth thought.

"Mornin', Macky," Fred chipped in between the lines in their anxious chorus, "just clearing this drain over here. But tell yer ma that she'll have to move the car if she wants me to rod it through, 'cos I'll have to lift that other drain cover over there. It's under the car, see? And I know I've got a good arm on me, but not strong enough to lift yer ma's car. Hah!"

Macbeth stared at him, hardly understanding a word of what old Fred was saying.

Duffy and Lennox pushed past Macbeth. One or two of the team were stirring by now, spread out in sleeping bags and under duvets in the living room.

Duffy and Lennox carried on their stream of worry:

"Why didn't you set an alarm, or something?"

"You knew you had to get up."

"Oi, Dunk, wake up!"

Mum appeared in doorway between the kitchen and the living room, gently smoothing back her hair. She couldn't smooth the twitch out of that right eye, so she turned and put on a kettle.

On previous such occasions, it had been Dunk's job to set the alarm and wake up the rest. He was awake now and just trying to figure out what was going on ... when a phone buzzed.

Someone was getting a message.

This is it, thought Macbeth. *This is really it.*

Duffy saw it, lying on the floor between the blankets and sleeping bags, and casually picked it up. He was just about to say, "Whose phone's this?" when – he couldn't resist it – he glanced down and read the incoming message.

Then he read it again.

"Oi!" Duncan called out. "What you doing?

That's my phone."

Duncan reached out for it.

Duffy pulled it away from his reach.

"And don't read my messages! GIVE IT HERE!"
Duncan yelled.

By now, the morning groans and chat had
stopped. Everyone stopped to look and listen to this
row that was growing in front of their eyes. Why
was Duffy behaving like a jerk, not letting Dunk
have his phone?

Then Duffy read out the message to everyone:
"Great stuff, Duncan. You're so right, Shotfield are
finished. No need for a trial. We know you're very
good. Fantastic to have you in the academy."

There was a split second of thought before the
horror kicked in. Then it was the wave of anger
from the players that hit Duncan, then a second
wave was Duncan screaming back at them that it
wasn't him.

"Hell, Dunk! What did you do that for?"

"You've always said that it's all for the team and
… and … and…"

"Yeah – look what you did to Cawd!"

"And all the time, it's you!"

In amongst this volley, Macbeth knew that he would have to join in, or it would look very strange if he just stood there, so he drummed up the energy to shout a "Yeah!" and a "Too right!" But then, just out of the corner of his eye, he noticed that Malcolm was looking at him. And looking at him some more.

Duncan was beyond furious, beyond upset, and was beginning to tear up. "It wasn't me!" he kept saying. "Someone else has done this…" But his words were getting lost in the row and he wasn't getting a hearing.

Mum had finished boiling the kettle but, as Macbeth noticed through the doorway, she hadn't actually made any tea or coffee with it and now she stood in the doorway. He watched her take in a deep breath: "What's up, lads? What's going on?"

Macbeth felt impressed at just how cool she seemed to be when she said it. How did she keep her face looking so innocent?

Duffy started blurting it all out: he repeated the phone message and followed it straight after with an indignant, furious, outraged rant about Duncan, while Duncan by now had stopped trying to answer and was just heaving in dry sobs.

"Oh no!" Mrs Macbeth said, her voice dripping with disappointment. "Oh dear! And after all the work you put in, lads. Really, Duncan. You've let everyone down."

Macbeth looked at her. Not a twitch in sight.

Duffy, standing close by, switched from his ranting tone and instead said to her kindly, "Don't worry yourself about it, Mrs Mack."

An inner smile crept behind Macbeth's eyes... If only Duffy knew!

But Macbeth saw that for Duncan, his mother's words were the last straw. What she said – and the fact that she didn't wait to hear his side of the story – was too much.

Duncan screamed at everyone in one horrible, unforgiving yell, grabbed his bag and phone, rammed on his tracky bottoms and shoes and stormed out of the house, still roaring and swearing.

Mrs Macbeth looked horrified at the swearing and left the room, sighing, "As if it's not bad enough that he did those things, and then that kind of language. In my house…"

Macbeth admitted to himself he was both shocked and amazed all in one. Not by the chaos that he and his mother had let loose, but by watching and hearing his mother putting on a show as cool and as calculated as this. *How does she do it?* he asked himself.

The room was in a mess in many ways at the same time: a mess of blankets, duvets and sleeping bags across the floor; bags, boots, shin pads scattered about between them. But there was also the mess of the team – so recently feeling so united, so full of themselves for winning the Youth Cup, but now full of anger, sadness and suspicion. Macbeth looked round the room at them. He kept his head down, his eyes half-closed, but all the while sneaking a look through his eyelashes at how it was playing out.

He imagined that some would be wondering why Duncan had done such a thing. There would be others, like Malcolm and Donal, who were probably wondering if Duncan had perhaps been telling the truth: *had* someone played some kind of awful trick on him? He saw how close they sat to each other.

An unheard whisper passed through the room – or was it purely in his mind? – if Duncan had been tricked, who by? And why?

Mrs Macbeth came back into the room, wiping her hands on a towel. Again and again. "I think you lads are going to have to pull yourselves together. Remember: you're still a team. You've got great players. And you have a great assistant coach – even though I say it myself." She laughed in a slightly embarrassed way.

Mack waved to her in the way that players wave when the fans at big matches call out their names, hoping it looked natural.

"There's still just time to grab a slice of toast, boys. You can't play on an empty stomach, so…"

Malcolm and Donal stood up. Donal had tears in his eyes now.

"Look, guys ... we're sorry," Malcolm said, "I don't think ... we're not ... er..."

Macbeth figured quick as a flash that they must have been chatting to each other. He could see that the others were sitting quietly, watching and listening, wondering what was coming next. He guessed the mood: they were thinking, was this the end of Shotfield, right here and right now? After all they'd been through, that great draw they squeezed out on a freezing Sunday morning in the mud back in November? And that time Banksy battled through with one eye closing up from a clash of heads with that crazy nutter guy from Grisewold Youth?

"It's just that ... there's something that's not quite ... er..." Malcolm couldn't finish what he was trying to say because he couldn't finish what he was thinking.

Macbeth looked from Malcolm to Donal and back again.

Donal filled in: "We'd rather not play today, and

I think we're..." He tailed off.

"...leaving." Malcolm finished.

They both silently pulled on their outdoor clothes, slipping them over the T-shirts and boxers they had slept in, and slouched out of the room and out of the house.

CHAPTER 10

Rossi

*I*t was a disunited bunch that legged it down the road to get to the game. Instead of the usual tight group, laughing, playing tricks and thumping each other on the shoulders, they were stretched out along the road like dying leaves hanging on a winter tree, some walking on their own, looking at the ground, some in silent pairs.

Rossi was looking at his phone. His granddad was texting him some stuff about what a weird night it had been: his granddad had thought he had heard a screaming sound, rushed downstairs and found that Tiggy had killed a mouse.

What a great mouser he is!
Best of luck with the game, love Granddad.

As Rossi read it, he found it chimed with something he had dreamed in the night: a car alarm had gone off – not because someone had tried to get in, but because the car had, all on its own, with no one in it, started to move down a hill... On and on it went, till it crashed at the bottom. The car was a write-off, as Granddad would have said: "A write-off, Rossi, me lad." And as Rossi brought the wreck into his mind, he realized that in his dream it was *Dunk's* car – well, his family's car...

He put his phone back in his pocket and walked on, feeling more uneasy than ever. Then, he heard footsteps getting closer, so he swung his head round and was glad to see that it was Duffy. Rossi noticed that he was panting and scratching at a sore patch behind his ear.

After a bit, Rossi asked, "Do you think Dunk really did that? You know, wrote that stuff?"

"Seems like it," Duffy said, looking at Rossi straight in the face.

Rossi had a sense that they each had something to say, but neither of them were sure whether it was a good idea to say it. He nodded.

"But then..." Duffy stopped himself going on. They walked on some more. The others were out of earshot. "Bit odd that Malcolm and Donal cleared off like that."

Rossi dived in: "What do you mean? You don't think they..." They were like two dogs, sniffing at each other, Rossi thought.

"I mean it's odd. That's all," Duffy answered.

This hint – was it a clue? – walked along with them.

"Well," Rossi muttered, "if they're not willing to hang in there, then it's best if Mack takes Dunk's place. I'd've said either of them would have been the best as coach, but..."

"You think?" said Duffy sharply.

Rossi wasn't sure he liked the way Duffy said that, sharp and suspicious, so he just murmured something that Granddad always said – "Hey ho, make the best of a bad job and live to see another day" – whatever that meant. They had all been such good friends before, a real team.

And now, Rossi thought, *none of us know what the other is really thinking.*

They walked on.

CHAPTER 11

Banksy

*a*s the team gathered for the game, they were each in their own bubble, thinking their own thoughts, each troubled in their own way about what had happened. Banksy, usually so calm, could feel himself churning over inside. He looked across at Mack.

Huh! It's all come right for you, hasn't it? he thought. Just as those three weird guys in the mist had said. *First you take Cawd's place, then Dunk's. Did you wangle that to happen? Did you arrange it in some way or another that I can't figure out?*

But then, he had another thought: *Well, if things are panning out just how those weird guys said, then, didn't they say some stuff about me? About how I would get my turn?*

Or did I just imagine that? What did they say? What did they really, really say? he asked himself desperately, trying to find it in his mind. It made him uneasy, though. He felt his stomach. It was hopping. A sick feeling. Maybe it would be better if he sat out the first few minutes, to see if the feeling would go away, and ask Mack to sub him on if it calmed down.

The others were stuffing their shin pads down their socks, double-tying their laces, and starting to do their stretches.

He didn't notice that Mack and his mum had drifted up to him.

Macbeth

Banksy didn't look so good, Macbeth thought to himself, doing a sideways glance at his mother. "Hey, Banksy, how's it going?"

"Hey, look, Mack," Banksy said, "I'm feeling a bit yuck. I think I'm going to throw up. Is it OK if I sit out the first few minutes, see how I feel, and if it's all OK, come on a bit later?"

Mum took control in a way that irritated Macbeth: "Sure, Banksy, that'll be fine, but I think you will be OK. It's not as if you've gone green or anything!" She laughed and added, "I think it'd be great for you to play once you feel better." She put her hand on Banksy's arm.

Macbeth was looking at his phone:

"Just had a text from my cousin who says that Malcolm and Donal have had the OK from Angles to go and trial for them."

Snakes! he thought. *What is the matter with them? Snakes!* But he kept his cool.

Mum, too, cool and calm, helped Banksy put his

jacket on so he wouldn't get cold.

Macbeth picked up from Mum and, speaking in the tone of a true captain, said, "Yeah, Banksy, take it easy. I've had that sick thing before. It just goes, yeah?" He winked, made his hand into a fist, punched it forward into mid-air in a show of friendship. "Stick with it, Banksy!"

And Banksy slowly made his way off to the touchline, skipping the warm-ups.

"OK, let's do these stretches, guys!" Macbeth shouted to the rest. And everyone got to work on their quads, hamstrings, groins and the rest.

For a moment, it felt to Macbeth like it had all come good. Wasn't this what he had always wanted? He had heard the top players saying on TV that, sure, it's about talent, and, sure, it's about hard work, but there's also that extra thing – there's no name for it, call it "luck", call it "coincidence", call it "fate", or whatever – but that's what gets you noticed; how on that particular day in that particular place, someone important gets to spot you. Spot YOU! Fate or not, you've got to do anything – anything at all – to make that happen. Running a team, the best team, with no adult coach, just as he was right now, was the best place to be. The very best. Hero.

He looked at them warming up. Perhaps, though, they were doing it without the push he'd seen from them before. Perhaps. And he looked into the middle distance, and saw Banksy strolling towards the touchline of pitch eight. The other pitches in this huge park were filling up with their players, the splash of their kits, red, blue, yellow, maroon bobbing about like bright little boats on a green sea. He saw Banksy, far off now, looking across to pitches four and five, and a thought dropped into Macbeth's head: *Who does he think he is? That look!* It seemed so ... what was it ... like he was the boss? Like he was some kind of boss-man strolling about between his teams.

And then Macbeth remembered that night in the mist on the common. Oh, sure, the three weird guys had told him, Macbeth, how one day he was going to be great, but in a way, hadn't they said the same thing about Banksy ... just that Banksy was a bit younger, or something? *What was that they said about sparks and fires?* He felt a strong pulse of resentment rise in his throat. *Were they saying that somehow Banksy was better than him? Was that their point? What – and I'm some sort of stand-in guy just so that Banksy – the real talent – would take over? Was that what they meant?*

Macbeth's mind raced along with the logic of it. He didn't need to say it, it was obvious: it was Banksy next. He was the next in line to take over. *Hah! The sly dog.* Macbeth watched him, far off now, wandering on. *The sly, sly dog. Banksy's known it all along.* Just biding his time, for a moment when he could slide him, Macbeth, out of the picture. *I wonder what he's got planned...*

At that, in a flash, Macbeth had it figured: *Don't wait for Banksy to plan something. Get him first!* Then he checked himself. *No, I can't do that. I can't. Not good old solid Banksy. He's never done me any harm.* And then straight afterwards, like photos on his phone sliding over each other, came the opposite thought: *Do I want to be a pro? Do I want to be in that place, in that time, where I, just me, get noticed? Yes! Then do it, Macky Boy, do it!*

But what?

He dawdled over to the guys warming up.

"Hey, guys, that's great. Real great. I'm ... er ... just going over to check everything's OK with the ... er ... ref... Not sure who's doing it today. Y'know, like ... er ... Dunk used to do..."

He sensed that he was talking too much and stopped himself. He waved at them and started walking over to the table where the refs for the day stood. He knew he was going to say something, but what he was actually going to say hadn't fully come into shape in his mind.

Halfway there, he saw that a ref was coming towards him. *Well, here was the chance, surely.* Wasn't all this part of the bigger picture he was thinking about – luck, chance, fate or whatever it is going on?

"Hey!" Macbeth said to the guy as he got near.

"Hey!" he said back. It was that same odd, stringy-looking guy they had reffing for them once before. "All set?" said the ref.

"Kind of," Macbeth said, feeling that surge that came to him whenever he started to plan ahead, scheme and plot.

"There's a problem?" asked the ref in a way that suggested that if even if there was a problem, he didn't want to hear it.

"Yep, look, I know it's not your issue, but I got a guy in the team who is basically wrecking it. He's doing everything he can to break it up."

"Uh-huh."

"No, look, I know it's none of your business, but you remember Dunk?"

"Uh-huh."

Macbeth lowered his voice. "This guy I'm talking about, Banksy, he got into Dunk's phone, put in some message about Dunk wanting to play for Angles, sent it to Angles and it all came out, and at the time we thought it really was Dunk who did it. I still can't prove it, but..."

The ref was massaging his right thigh in a very attentive way.

"Hey, I can see you're not that interested in what I'm saying, but the team's falling apart. The fallout from the Dunk thing is people thought it was Malcolm and Donal – do you remember them? – and they've gone. I'm telling you that Banksy shouldn't be in the game."

"Have you reported this to the league committee?" the ref said.

Macbeth felt the situation ebbing away from him. He wasn't getting through. *For goodness' sake,* he felt like saying to the ref, *it's down to you: red card him. Get him off. Get rid of him!* But Macbeth knew he couldn't be that direct. Or could he? What if this guy was bent? *What if...?* Another idea shot into his mind.

"Hey," Macbeth said in as honest a way as he could manage, "at least you know what's going on, and I know how you refs come out even in weather like this, and all you get for it is our subs. You spend it all on a cup of tea and a burger, eh? It's next to nothing."

"Yeah."

"All for the love of the game, right?"

"Yeah."

"That's what I'm saying. Banksy hasn't got that. He's in it for something else, some kind of bad stuff. We can't let him go on like this. Do you think there's any way, for the good of the game, you could..."

"What?"

"If there was a way you could make sure that ...

that … he doesn't stay on the pitch, if you get me."

The ref started noticing his other thigh now and was giving that a good old workover with his fingertips. He looked up. "I like going out with my mates after the game," he said.

Macbeth picked up on this straightaway. It was just the moment he had been wondering about. "Well, if things work out," he said, "you could nip into our place on the way to see your mates and I can … er … y'know, make sure you've got enough for the evening."

"Got you," the ref said in the most promising voice so far in the conversation.

"The last house on Raven Avenue, if you're walking from here," Macbeth said, "number fifty-two."

"Done," said the ref.

"Done," Macbeth chipped in.

They shook on it.

Macbeth turned and walked back towards the team. *You're on your way, Banksy,* he said to himself.

CHAPTER 12

Mrs Macbeth

By the time Mrs Macbeth got to the game, it was half-time. She stood in the Hub to get out of the cold. She usually got out there to watch the games, but with a northerly wind blowing up, it felt like it was halfway to the Arctic out there. At half-time on days like this, some of the teams came back to the Hub so they didn't cool down too much.

As she stamped the ground to get the blood flowing through her feet, she wondered about the hundreds of young people out there playing. Which ones really would make it to the top? She felt that catch in her throat as she thought of her Macky and that one day it could be him. She laughed at herself, as she saw her own image in her mind's eye being a football mum in a big stadium, Wembley even, as a grown-up Macky was climbing the steps to collect a medal from some famous person or other, the Queen even...

Her little dream was interrupted by the team clomping into the Hub, their studs thumping on the concrete floor. She scanned their faces to see how it was going. Were they up? Down? Even-stevens? Anything dramatic happened?

They seemed chirpy enough. She looked from the team to Macky and back. He was sitting to one side, breathing heavily. But then, she thought, something felt odd. Something was missing. *Banksy!* Where was Banksy?

She looked into Macky's face. "Where's Banksy?" she whispered, "and why aren't you sitting with the others?"

"There was some bother. Leave it, Mum."

"Where is he?" she repeated.

"Things happen, for goodness' sake. You don't have to know everything all the time. There's some stuff going on, and it's OK. I don't know, what with Dunk not being here. He's well out of it anyway."

Mrs Macbeth couldn't make head nor tail of this. "Hey, Macky, shake out of it. You're starting to talk nonsense."

She put herself closer to his ear. "We're going to have a bit of a spread later on, everyone's invited, so make sure there's no long face, eh?"

"Sure, sure," Macky said in an unconvincing way, "and be nice to Banksy, eh?"

"Of course, why wouldn't I? Where is he?"

Again, no straight answer came from him.

She looked out through the double doors of the Hub. Dense cloud filled the sky; it could almost be evening. She urged the boys out again.

Macbeth

Macbeth stepped out into the darkening air, and took in a gulp of breath. It felt like he was swallowing the night. For the rest of the game, it was going to be a contest between the light from the lamps and the oncoming dark. He felt his mother step up behind him.

"It's going to be all right," he said. He winked at her and ran on towards pitch eight.

CHAPTER 13

Banksy

*R*age would be too weak a way of saying it, Banksy thought. *One tackle! It wasn't even high! OK, it was a bit studs out, but that happens ten times a game. It was a yellow at most. If that! If that!*

He was furiously stamping down the long, lonely road towards his home.

All because of that useless, stringy, mean-faced nerd-head of a ref. And now he was out of the game, and out of the next two games.

The ref's face seemed to leer into his as he walked. First the smirk, the card coming out of the pocket, the little nod, the turn away. He saw it again and again as he walked. The smirk. The card. The nod. The turn.

And as he thought, and walked to the rhythm of the smirks and cards, he felt himself walking towards ... who? Who was it ... Mack? Mack was there in his mind, just as he, Banksy, walked towards the touchline and on to the Hub. And what was the look on Mack's face? Did he come over and put his arm round him? No. Did he complain to the ref? No.

He just stood looking at me, Banksy thought, *leaving me on my own. And that expression on his face: like … like … like he agreed with that nerd-head ref. Like it really was a foul and it was fair that I got a red for it. Was it, though? Was it? NO!!! And Mack, you sided with him! Yes, you did. Yes, you darn well did!!!*

Banksy pounded the pavements. He went on as if he was talking to Macbeth: *And you had the beginnings of a smile, a little curl at the corner of your mouth, didn't you, Mack? You did. I saw it. You did, didn't you? Well, I can tell you, I'm out. I'm out of it. Whatever's going on with this team is sick. And I don't want to be part of it. I'm gone. I'm finished. You won't see me again.*

He pulled his phone out of his pocket, banged the keys, and texted his old friend, Mike Fleet.

Hey, Fleety, am comn over. Yu no how yu wntd 2 join Shots. Dont. Stay out ov it. Tell yu mor 18er.

CHAPTER 14

Macbeth

*M*acbeth led the boys up the path in front of his house, the boot studs clattering on the concrete. Mum had gone on ahead to get things ready. As the others wrestled with getting their boots off by the door, Macbeth slipped into the kitchen.

"Don't say anything about anything," Macbeth whispered at her fiercely.

"Mm?" her eyebrows lifted, questioning such a strange ask, and a twitch followed.

"You know what I mean," he said. "I'll help with the food."

He slid out of the kitchen and upstairs into his room, closing the door softly behind him. He opened his wardrobe, pushed aside his old shoes that were lying on the floor inside, and revealed a small locked metal box. He pulled a key out of on old boot, opened the box, took out some folded twenty-pound notes and slipped them into his pocket. A flash of a picture popped into his mind of a time he had walked into Mum's room and seen her scrabbling about with some pills in a drawer. How awkward she was that he had seen her. And how they both pretended that he hadn't. Then the picture went. He scrambled the shoes and boots over the top, closed the wardrobe and nipped out of the room. As he moved back downstairs, Macbeth felt pleased he was doing things so neatly and quickly.

The rest of the team were sitting down and making appreciative sighs at the sight of his mum's sandwiches, crisps and cakes.

"Oh, I've forgotten the dips, Macky," she said, and Mack sidled out into the kitchen to pick them up.

The doorbell rang.

"I'll get it!" he called out to anyone and everyone.

At the door stood the gangly ref, his hoody pulled over his face. There was a moment's pause as they looked at each other.

The ref shrugged. "I did it, didn't I?"

Macbeth put his hand in his pocket.

"Like you said, a red," the ref added.

Macbeth handed him the folded-over notes.

The ref turned and muttered over his shoulder. "Don't know what's going on with you lot, but my guess is it won't end there."

"Yeah, yeah," Mack said, more to the ground than to the ref, but in his mind, the ref's little throwaway thought – "it won't end there" – set him thinking of how getting Banksy out of it could, if he wasn't careful, just kick off more stuff ... like, like ... how having a haircut doesn't stop your hair growing. Then, thinking this annoyed him. One moment, getting Banksy out of it felt good, and the next, here he was tying himself in knots thinking how it could all get worse. Knots and more knots. It was maddening.

Mum appeared behind him as he shut the front door. "Come on, Macky, you should be in there. Looks a bit odd you're not tucking in with everyone else. I've set your place up the window end."

"Yeah, yeah, yeah, I know. I know," Mack said, his ratty, impatient tone cutting the air.

The guys were, just as Mum had said, tucking in. He looked at them, their faces only half-lit because

Mum had switched off the bright central light and had gone for what she called the "mood look": three low side lights in different corners of the room that left shadows like dark grey pools waiting here and there.

"You wanna get some of this," Lennox said to Mack, laughing, as he munched into another sandwich. He pointed at the empty chair where Mack was to sit.

"Do it," said Rossi.

"Don't look at me like that," Mack muttered.

Mack's words spun through the room. Faces turned towards him, showing shock and looks of "What now?", or "What's he talking about?" But Mack was peering at the place at the table where he was just about to sit down.

It was Banksy, wasn't it? Banksy must have come in, when he was upstairs, and sat down in his seat.

"Who let *him* in?" Mack looked round. He felt cornered. Were people ganging up on him?

Mrs Macbeth took it all in: the boys' faces, Macbeth peering at his chair. "Oh, sorry, boys."

She put her hand on Macbeth's forehead and then immediately put it to her own forehead. "Temperature," she muttered below her breath, and then more clearly, "he's not well, lads. I've seen this before – ever since he was little. These little moments can come on really quickly, stay where you are. Please, lads, don't stare at him. We learned a long time ago, it seems to make it worse."

She expertly swivelled Macbeth round and guided him into the kitchen and shut the door behind them. She turned on him, bending towards him furiously. "What the hell do you think you're doing? Staring like some crazy person at an empty chair. Some of them will get what's going on. Never make it easy for people to read your mind, do you hear me?"

Macbeth gestured back into the room. "He's there. He's sitting there. It's like ... like he gets the red card, walks off, and then ... comes back on!"

"You're talking nonsense, Macky! Shake out of it! For goodness' sake, get a hold of yourself," she said, and, as if not trusting him to do it himself, she shook him. It seemed to work: his face cleared, and she guided him back towards the room.

Again, Macbeth peered towards his place at the table, and this time it seemed clear. The sound of teeth on crisps and Doritos crackled.

"Hah!" Macbeth said to everyone, as if to laugh the whole thing off. "We're good, aren't we?"

"Yeah," a few unenthusiastic noises came back.

"And, look, it's a real pity that Banksy's … y'know … not here. He took that sending off really badly."

Macbeth looked round, trying to scan their faces in the low, shadowy light of Mum's "mood look". But then, as he did so, wasn't that … wasn't that … *Bansky* again? Wasn't that him in the corner where the lava lamp silently blooped its red bubbles?

He waved his arm in that direction as if he was flapping away a disgusting smell. He raised his voice. "Get out of here!"

His mum dived in quick: "Don't worry about it, lads." She put her arm round Macbeth. "Like I said, he gets these moments. It sometimes spoils the occasion a bit ... but..." Her voice ebbed away. She smiled kindly at Macbeth and back to the boys.

Now Macbeth was shaking and pointing to the corner.

His mother pulled him close. "Don't! Just don't, do you hear me?" she said.

Macbeth looked up at his mother. "See that? Now he's gone." He smiled with a look of pride, as if it were he who had rid the room of this awful thing.

Mrs Macbeth's voice smoothed and quietened: "Now, come on, Macky, you don't want to spoil the fun. You're making *me* see things now!" and she giggled, trying to make it all seem like some funny little thingy that didn't matter.

Rossi butted in. "What you seeing, Mack?"

The others, with their looks, seemed to be asking the same question: what was Mack seeing? What was he looking at, exactly?

Mrs Macbeth wouldn't let him answer. She was in between Rossi and Macbeth like a ref in a boxing match. "Please, lads, like I said, don't stare at him. Don't ask him questions. It just makes it worse."

She looked round the room, their faces half-lit by the corner lamps, their hands moving in and out of the shadows.

"Look, I'm really sorry, boys. I'm really, really sorry, but I think it would be best if you went. These little moments he has can get worse. I remember once... Oh, look, it doesn't matter now, but I think it's best if you go. I'll probably have to call the doctor..."

The boys moved their chairs back, slowly got to their feet, clearly unwilling to give up so soon on the cake and buns and chocolate fingers.

"Sorry, lads, keep moving. Don't hang about."

They did just that, some of them looking seriously spooked.

Lennox did the right thing: "I hope he gets better soon, Mrs Mack."

The others murmured their agreement and scrambled towards their boots, half-putting them on and stumbling out of the door into the night.

"Have a good evening, boys," Mrs Macbeth threw after them.

Once the door closed behind them, she turned back to Macbeth.

He was slumped on the sofa, grumbling to himself: "You start doing stuff like this, and it leads to more stuff and more stuff and … and…"

He snapped out of it for a moment. "What's the time, Mum?"

"Late. Later than it was. And a bit earlier than it will be later on." It was one of her jokes.

"And where was Duffy? Why wasn't he here?" Mack asked her as if she ought to have known.

"Did you tell him we were having something to eat together?" she said, glad that at least now he was making some sort of sense, instead of the gibberish he was talking before.

But then he went back to his muttering: "I better keep an eye on him… Find out what he's doing. I don't like that he wasn't here…"

"What's that, dear?" His mum tried to keep control, but he was off on another tack straightaway.

"I'm going to see if I can find those three scouts that me and Banksy met that time."

Mum looked at him full in the face.

Macbeth figured she hadn't remembered. "You know, the guys I met after the game when I tackled that Andersen kid…"

The mention of the tackle brought to mind the moment, the sound of his foot on Andersen's leg, the blood that dripped out of his knee…

"You really are out of sorts, Macky," she said with real concern in her voice.

"I think I had better lie down," he said, his words slowing down. "This headache is killing me."

CHAPTER 15

Macbeth

*F*ar off, at the end of a long dark tunnel, stood the three men, their faces hidden. He called out to them, but no sound came out of his mouth. He tried to make a move towards them, but his body wouldn't budge. There was a whirring sound in his ears, like the sound of air con mixed with the long, drawn-out note of a bass in a band. He knew this was dangerous – all the more so because he couldn't move his feet – but he didn't know *why* it was dangerous. It just *felt* dangerous. If there was one thing about him that was moving, it was his heart. He could feel it in his ears. He tried to wave to the men, but his arm stayed by his side. It felt as if his mind was like pools of dark water lying in a road. He tried to shake them up, but the water didn't move.

The whirring bass sound gave way to rushing air that he could feel on his face. In the flow, a fourth man appeared and stood with the others. All of them huddled together now, they started mumbling to each other. He strained all he could to hear it. There was a moment when they all looked towards him, pointed at him and turned back.

Slowly, he started to make it out. It was if they were so far away, on the other side of the universe or something, that there was a delay between when they spoke and when he could hear what they were saying. The guy who had just turned up was angry. He was saying something about what did they think they were doing, talking to Macbeth without bringing him in on it. Either he was boss, or he wasn't. There was a gap in the talk into which pushed more rushing air, and then the boss started again, while still Macbeth couldn't move, and stayed stuck to the spot as if someone had fixed him there. The boss was urging them to meet up again and meet. *Meet me?* Mack asked himself. *Did they say that?* Mack felt the pools of dark water in his mind move at last, as he realized that yes, this boss wanted them to meet him.

He heard laughter. Laughter far off in the tunnel. Was it them, or was it from beyond them, wherever and whatever that was? And amongst this jeering sound he heard, "He's lost it."

And another more sneering voice said, "The harder they fall…"

The harder they fall? he felt himself asking. *What does that mean? Why don't they say what it means?* And this seemed to stir him. Just asking the question seemed to give him the power to move. But the moment he had that power, it spread to the scene in front of him. The moment he could begin to make himself heard, the scene started to fade.

He waved. It was no use, they were disappearing into thin air, so he called out, "What's that even mean? Eh? Well?"

Mum was standing by his bed. "You're shouting, Macky," she said.

"Am I?" he said, peering into the gloom of his room. "What does what mean?" He lay on his back staring at the ceiling. No. It was gone. He couldn't remember. He rolled over on to his side. "Hey, Mum, that thing that people say, 'The harder they fall'. What's that all about?"

"It's something people say when you think you're better than you are," she replied. "Or you'll come a cropper. Ever heard that?"

"Come a cropper? No."

"Oh, it's like you're heading for a crash."

Macbeth didn't reply. He shut his eyes again. He heard Mum go out of the room, and the darkness flowed over him.

CHAPTER 16

Lennox

ossi stayed at Lennox's place that night, and in the morning they stood by the toaster as they stuffed in slice after slice, spreading Nutella, wolfing one down and on to the next.

"Odd, isn't it?" Lennox said through the crumbs. "Hey, but you know that."

Rossi nodded. It looked to Lennox that he would have said something, but Rossi was still chewing.

"I mean," Lennox went on, "it's not as if we haven't noticed that Dunk's out of it, Banksy's out of it."

Rossi managed a "Mm" and a nod.

"And why would Malcolm and Donal have done that?" Lennox wondered. "I don't get it. I don't get it." He shook his head as if shaking it would get the truth out.

Rossi put another slice in the toaster, still chewing away.

"I think … it's eating up Mack. He can't bear what's happening. He's the good guy in all this, isn't he?"

Rossi didn't answer. Lennox glanced at him. Was Rossi not answering because he agreed with him? Or because he disagreed with him? Or because he was wondering whether to switch from Nutella to Marmite?

Lennox tried another tack. "And Duffy. Where's he in all this?"

Rossi finally answered, "Yeah, well, Malcolm's off with Angles now, isn't he? Duffy too, I s'pose. They're well out of it. None of that spooky stuff with Mack seeing things in the dark. Sheesh, that wound me up, that did. Whoa!"

Lennox paused. "Duffy's gone to Angles too?"

Rossi seemed to be concentrating on the Marmite, spreading it to the very edge of the slice. "It's what I heard." The knife scraped on the hard surface of the toast. "He won't regret it," he added as the scraping came to a stop.

Lennox watched Rossi's hand. It felt like they were both moving towards the same spot. "If only someone … like … went over to Angles and tried to get them back, or something?" he said dreamily, his voice turning his thought into a question.

Rossi nodded.

Lennox was now a bit more certain that Rossi was on his side. "Sheesh, everything's falling apart with him running the team."

I wonder if Rossi noticed I said "him" and I didn't say Mack, Lennox thought.

The toaster popped another slice. It had been in too long. It was burnt.

Lennox picked it up and threw it in the bin.

CHAPTER 17

Macbeth

"**D**ouble or quits!"

It was late, and Macbeth was standing outside a room at the back of the snooker hall on the high street. He had his ear to the door. Earlier, he had asked at the leisure centre whether anyone knew of three guys who scouted for the academies. Mrs Grant on the counter had said she thought she did and then had given him an address. But was it the right one? And did she really know anyway? Apparently, these three were quite well known. Or so she said. Where he stood now, a worn carpet lay on the floor and a picture of a long-forgotten conjuror hung from the wall. Weird, or what? A long crack ran from the ceiling down to the floor. *Maybe lightning has hit this place,* Macbeth thought.

He could hear some people from inside, laughing in a jeering way that sounded familiar to him. He knocked on the door.

"Come!" shouted a voice.

Once inside, Macbeth could see that they were playing cards. He tasted the smoke from their cigarettes in his mouth, and it hung in the air around them, blurring their faces. *Talent scouts who smoke?* he thought to himself. *How does that work? Creeps.*

He glanced around the room, looking at their faces. There was something similar about them. Were they brothers? Same floppy skin under their eyes, same floppy hair down the sides of their faces.

They all nodded to each other. No need for introductions.

"There's a couple of things I want to check up on," Macbeth said. "I mean, like, seeing that you seem to know so much about what goes on before it even happens."

"Do we?" said the one with the floppiest hair.

The others sniggered.

One was shuffling the pack of cards. "Go ahead, son," he said.

"I just want to know—"

They didn't wait for him to finish. One whispered to the other, "Hear him out, but don't say a thing."

A voice came from the back of the room, but he couldn't see who was speaking: "Just watch that Duffy, son."

Macbeth jolted. *Who was that?* he thought. Then he noticed someone he had missed before, standing in the dark, up against the wall.

The figure spoke again, and its voice hardly seemed to be coming from a real person: "You'll be OK, son. No one's going to bother you. No one's got it in them to challenge you."

Mack felt a little kick of triumph inside to hear

that, but then the voice added, "Leastways not anyone with a name."

Sweet, he thought. *Everyone's got a name.* He had never met anyone who didn't have a name. *Nothing to worry about there. Move on.*

The one who was shuffling the cards now put the pack down on the table with a smack. He cut the pack, flipped the one half on to the other and went on shuffling.

Even so, Macbeth thought, *he said to watch out for Duffy. Right! I will. Think, Macky boy, you're going to need to come up with something that'll take him out of the picture too. Next game, perhaps...*

The figure seemed to have heard what Macbeth was thinking because it answered his thoughts: "Don't worry about him, son. So long as you carry on using the same training base, you're in the clear."

Macbeth smiled to himself. *Move the training base? As if!* They had a really great deal with Mrs Grant and the people who ran it. *They wouldn't move in a hundred years. So that's sorted too.*

The three men sitting round the table made a move as if to say that they wanted to get on with the card game, but Macbeth had one more question:

"What about Banksy? He'll be back when he's served his red."

The shadowy figure who Macbeth was thinking of as the Voice moved slightly, and Macbeth could see a TV remote in his hand. A screen next to him came to life. In the light from the screen, Macbeth caught sight of the man's face. He wondered if it was the face in the dream, or perhaps had he met him before. *More pictures sliding over each other. So annoying.*

On to the screen came a vid of Banksy, but he was older and bigger. The players were in a different kit from usual. He strained to make it out. It was Palace Academy! He had made it! A feeling of envy and anger crept through Mack as he stared into the screen. There Banksy was, in the midst of what looked like young pros, passing the ball about, slick as you like, on a training pitch somewhere. Then there was some kind of penalty shoot-out training session. The players were a long way off from the camera, and the only sound you could hear came from the person who must have been holding the phone: a hoarse breathing noise. Macbeth could just make out that as they ran up, each one who scored got high-fives from Banksy, like they were the real up-and-coming stars or something. *Where did this vid come from? Had someone made it to taunt him? Banksy himself? Or had this creepy Voice guy made it? I thought they were on my side, these people?*

He went on watching. Now Banksy strolled up and whacked the ball into the top corner.

Postage stamp! Top bins! As easy as you like. Banksy turned to the camera, his arms in the air, legs apart, and the others ran up to him, fist-pumping and high-fiving like crazy. And yet Macbeth could hardly hear them. Just the breathing. And then a voice from the man holding the phone: "That was great, Banksy. Great!" And the vid cut out.

Macbeth stood up. Inside he was saying, *I didn't need that. I didn't need to see that.*

"OK, I get the point," he said to the men, but they hardly noticed. While the vid had been playing, the guys at the table had slowly gone on dealing cards and were now on to the next game.

Macbeth turned and left.

He stepped out of the building into the car park next to the snooker hall. A single street light in the corner shone down. The buses nearby chased each other along the high street, lit up like cruise ships in a harbour.

As he headed home, past the shops pouring out the flavour of chips, kebabs and fried chicken, Macbeth suddenly realized Lennox had joined him. Where had he come from? Had Lennox seen that he was in that room at the back of the hall? What did Lennox know?

"Hi," Macbeth said to him.

"Hi," Lennox replied in the same voice.

"Wasn't expecting to see you here, Len. What's happening?"

"Nothing much," Lennox said, keeping step with Macbeth as they strode their way on down the high street towards the market.

"Nothing much?" Macbeth asked, trying to hide any suspicion.

"Oh, well, Duffy's gone." The comment

dropped from Lennox like it was nothing more than a screwed-up paper bag.

"Has he?" Macbeth said, with real worry in his voice. "What d'you mean, 'gone'?"

"I dunno, man," said Lennox, "I heard that he's gone with Angles as well."

No, no, no, no, Macbeth said to himself. *I was going to deal with him myself. I see what's happening here. Yes! They're all going to Angles until we fall apart and that way they can just take over Shotfield. Wipe me out. They want to take it away from me. And I should have sorted Duffy earlier. What's the matter with me? I need to handle these things quicker. Right, get on with it.* He curled his fingers into a fist and punched his other hand.

"You all right?" he heard Lennox say to him.

"Sure," Macbeth said, "sure," and did what it took to smile – but really it was just a twitch that pulled his lips back.

He hoped that what Lennox saw in the dark was a grin.

CHAPTER 18

Mrs Duffy

Mrs Duffy scrabbled through the packets of biscuits and cookies in the sweet biscuit section at Sainsbury's.

"Jammie Dodgers, Jammie Dodgers," she murmured under her breath, "they must be here somewhere." One thing she didn't want was Duffy moaning at her later on, going on and on about how she hadn't got the right biscuits. Was she like that, when she was a kid, she wondered? *Have things changed? Are kids today so wrapped up in themselves that it's got to be the right everything or it's the end of the world? Do these kids of ours get more racked up than we used to? And they go in for more feuding, surely. It's like a war out there.* She smiled to herself. *Where are those darned Jammie Dodgers?* She really wanted to get this right.

What with her being so deep in thought, she hadn't noticed that her younger son, Brandon, had wandered off to the cereals and was getting ready to pounce on the Coco Pops.

Meanwhile, back at the biscuits, as her hand reached past the Oreos, Mrs Duffy became aware that someone else was pushing the biscuits.

It was Rossi.

That's nice, she thought, *one of Duffy's friends.* She always thought Rossi had a nice, trustworthy sort of a face. "Hello, Rossi, you hunting for the Jammie Dodgers too? Duffy would die for them."

"No," Rossi said, "I'm after the custard creams. Yum." He laughed.

"There," she said, pointing at them. "Hah! All right for you. I'm going to be in trouble now.

No Jammie Dodgers. Maybe *you* could tell him instead of me, and he won't be quite so cross!" She laughed at her own joke.

Rossi laughed back, but a bit awkwardly, and blurted out, "Actually, Mrs Duffy, I won't be seeing him at practice later on."

"Oh, I'm sorry," Mrs Duffy said, with an edge of worry.

"No. Erm. Perhaps he didn't tell you. But Duffy's gone off to Angles."

"Has he?" She raised her voice. "Has he?" She was standing up now, in the middle of the aisle.

An extremely old man asked her to move, leaned into the stacks, picked up a packet of plain digestives, tutted and muttered something about people coming into supermarkets to carry on their social life, and pushed his trolley off as if it was all the trolley's fault anyway.

She looked into Rossi's face. He looked just about the same as she felt – as if things weren't as they should be, but no one knew why.

She was cross and let Rossi hear about it. "Well,

he's let everyone down. Oh, I feel bad about that, I really do." She brushed her hair out of her eyes.

"Oh, no, I don't think so," Rossi said.

"I'm telling you," Mrs Duffy snapped back. "He has let the side down and—"

Rossi interrupted: "No, look. Duffy is one of the good guys. Really, he is. He wouldn't go for any old reason. He knows something's going on. Maybe he just thought that—" He stopped and looked down, staring at the chocolate digestives.

"What? Finish what you're saying."

"I dunno, maybe he thought that someone was out to get him, and he thinks he'll be better off out of it. It's all getting a bit weird at the moment."

Brandon bounced back with his Coco Pops.

"Oh, Brandon, I don't think they're very good for you. I thought we agreed that we would try to eat less sugary stuff."

Brandon held on to the Coco Pops.

Rossi looked at him. "A couple of carrots and a serving of broccoli – that's what you ought to be having for breakfast, Brandon mate."

"Duffy likes them," Brandon replied, "tell him I've got them."

"Well, actually…" Rossi was about to say more, but Mrs Duffy held up her hand. She didn't want him to go over the whole Angles story again.

"Yep," said Rossi bringing things to a close. "I'm off then. Hope you find the Jammie Dodgers. I've seen them in the corner shop, sometimes…"

"Bye, Rossi. Take care," Mrs Duffy said to him kindly. "Say goodbye, Brandon."

"Bye," Brandon said obediently but mechanically.

A woman closed in on them with a trolley piled high with half of Sainsbury's in it, as well as a baby stuck in the front who was howling and reaching out frantically, trying to catch the oat and raisin cookies.

"Well, well, well," Mrs Duffy said to herself more than to Brandon, "your brother's hopped it. He's chucked in Shotfield and gone to Angles."

She thought of Brandon standing on the touchline and cheering like mad for Shotfield over and over again. But then – *as he had also booed Angles over and over again, this was all going to get difficult,* she thought.

She looked at her watch. She was running late, her mother was due over in a minute and had lost the key.

As she was getting flustered about that, one of the Sainsbury's people came over and said, "Excuse me, if you're looking for the Jammie Dodgers, they're in with 'Party Time' today. The manager is trying a new party bay. If I were you, I would nip over there while there are still some to get." He winked.

Mrs Duffy pretended to not notice the wink, turned the trolley round and drove it fast towards "Party Time".

Brandon

Brandon, though, lingered. He had dropped the Coco Pops in the trolley, even though Mum had tried to block them, but now he was thinking about the Moon Bars that the manager had helpfully put next to the biscuits. Moon Bars? What, really? Real Moon Bars? *Really* real Moon Bars? His eyes were fixed on the neat little stack. He imagined himself opening up the packet and munching into ... a Moon Bar! *Mmm!*

But then, from nowhere, all of a sudden by his side stood two big boys. He looked up at them.

"Your bro's gone to Angles," one of them said.

Brandon nodded and looked back at the Moon Bar.

"Who do you want to play for?"

Brandon weighed it up. "Angles." Of course he did. He wanted to play with Duffy wherever he went.

"That's both of them," one boy said to the other. They stood looking at Brandon. One looked over his shoulder to see where Mrs Duffy had gone, and the other kneed Brandon in the side of the leg as hard as he could.

Brandon squealed and clutched his thigh. It was a dead leg. It had come at him so hard and fast that now he couldn't put his weight back on the leg.

One of the boys pointed his finger right into Brandon's face. He didn't need to say anything.

Brandon knew in an instant that it meant that more was coming if he didn't watch out. Then the boy's fingers went to his lips: he knew he'd better not say a word about this.

He heard Mum's voice from the next bay, "Brandon! You still there? Come on, I've got to get back. Nanna's coming over."

The boy menaced him again by looming over him.

He got the point: don't reply.

And then he picked up another message off the boy's face without either of them saying it: there was something coming for Duffy too. This was nasty. And serious. Brandon was shaking.

He thought he saw Mum's trolley coming round by the crisps and crackers. *She'll sort this,* he thought, but it was the old man back again. He had forgotten to get breadsticks. By the time Brandon turned round to look at the boys, they had gone.

He stood looking at where they could have run to, and then he felt his leg wobble. He swayed sidewise and grabbed the shelf next to him.

CHAPTER 19

Duffy

"Duffy listened to what Malcolm wanted. Malcolm was doing the Jimmy Bullock thing. It was a training routine Malcolm had seen ex-England player Jimmy Bullock do on *Soccer Now!* Malcolm had changed the routine to suit him: run to the halfway line, run back to the "D" and shoot! Doing it five times. He asked Duffy to roll the ball to him each time so that he could shoot.

He's testing me, Duffy thought. *He's trying to find out if I don't mind just being the guy who rolls the feed ball. Perhaps he's worried that I'm really arrogant. And that I'm thinking they'll be so well pleased I've come over to Angles that they'll put me straight into the first team. Or again, maybe they think I'm a flake and will nip back to Shotfield any time.*

He watched Malcolm as he ran back to the halfway line and fast towards the D.

Duffy rolled it, but it was clumsy and it bounced. Malcolm ran in on it, but because of the bounce, his foot got under the ball and he skied it over the bar.

Did he mean to do that? Duffy asked himself. He felt uneasy.

Now Malcolm was nodding towards the bench. Duffy picked up on it: this bit of the session was over.

On the way there, Malcolm said in a throwaway voice, "Decent place Angles are using here, eh?"

He gestured across the practice pitches, each of them with their artificial green shine.

Duffy nodded keenly.

They sat down, and Duffy couldn't stop himself talking immediately. "We're well out of it, man. It's all going crazy over there. Half the team are not talking to other half. People are not turning up to training. Or when they do turn up, they say that they feel sick and leave halfway through. It's crazy. One time, no one thought to bring the cones, so it meant we couldn't do dribbles properly. The ball we were supposed to use had a gash in the side of it, like someone had left it in the car park or something and a car had run over it. It's bad, Malcolm. It's bad."

Duffy hoped that Malcolm was getting it. He watched Malcolm look across at the new "Hub", at this centre: it was leaking the beautiful smell of muffins hot from the oven. *Mmm, great for snacking on later,* Duffy thought.

Malcolm said, "I'll be straight with you, Duffy. You know whose fault it is, don't you?"

Duffy knew only too well who Malcolm was talking about but for the moment said nothing. He didn't want to be the first to say. Neither did Malcolm, by the looks of it. Instead, it felt like the presence of Mack sat between them as the person they both knew in that moment as "the fault".

"I mean," Malcolm started to say in a hesitating sort of a way, "you got taken in by him, you—"

Duffy wasn't having this and moved to interrupt Malcolm. "Look, I didn't—"

But Duffy could hear that Malcolm wanted to go on and stopped him saying any more. "I mean, it's a bit kind of funny that Mack hasn't got you out of Shotfield. The way I see it is that you're still in with him, really." Malcolm motored on with this tack: "You could have come over to Angles just to get at me. How do I know you're not doing his dirty work for him?"

Duffy felt the challenge. He frowned. This wasn't easy. He looked at the scuffed surface at his feet where a thousand boots had stamped. "I'm not." His voice peaked. He knew it sounded nervous and weak.

Malcolm took it in. "Yeah," he said, "but I've seen how he works. Even good guys get taken in by him." He popped out a little laugh. "Actually, I'm not that good at spotting who's been taken in and who hasn't."

Duffy was desperate to stay onside and threw out a little laugh.

"You don't suppose Mack has got any other tricks he wants to play?"

Duffy's mind was racing ahead. He knew that this whole affair had sucked him in, turned him upside down, and now his thoughts were getting jumbled, full of suspicions and fears. He kept coming up with different scenarios as a way of explaining all the awful stuff that had happened. One moment they had been a great team, winning trophies, getting noticed by scouts and coaches, and then in a matter of weeks it had all turned to chaos, spite, anger.

"Mack hasn't come to some deal with you, has he? You know, he'll do you some kind of favour if you come over to Angles and mess things up here?"

Duffy felt his face flush. He raised his voice: "Hell, Malcolm. If you think that, then you don't know me."

Malcolm said nothing. Duffy could feel Malcolm watching him.

"And if you want to push me away, Malcolm, then it's like you're saying to Mack, 'Go ahead, Mack! You ruin a great team. You're boss. You deserve it!'"

Malcolm shrugged.

Well, if that's the way he thinks, Duffy thought. "I'm outta here, Malcolm," he said and stood up.

Malcolm flicked a bit of dried mud off his boot and said, "Take it easy. I'm not saying you're the pits." Duffy saw Malcolm glance at him out of the corners of his eyes. "I'm saying Shotfield is finished. It's a mess. And you know what? I'm going to take it back."

Wow! That was putting it out there. Great, Duffy thought. *Some action.* "That's good," he said. "Yes, Malcolm. Do it!"

"But I'll tell you something ..."

Now what? Duffy thought.

"... what if I'm no better than Mack? I mean, he's a better player than me, right? What if I took over Shotfield and that made the whole outfit worse? Could be. And then everyone will walk about saying, 'Wow, wasn't it great when Mack was running the team, all those runs from deep, all those assists. That Malcolm is rubbish!'"

Duffy felt himself being whirled around like when he was a little kid sitting in one of those whirling teacups at the fair. He shook his head and rubbed the space between his eyebrows.

"You know what I'm saying, Duffy," Malcolm went on. "Whatever you think of Mack – all the lies and tricks he's done to get himself to the top, now double that. That's me. I don't show it, but that is me."

As he said "that is me", Duffy watched how at each word Malcolm pointed to the ground as if he was so low he lived down there, in the ground, or even under the ground.

This wasn't at all how Duffy imagined it would be coming over to Angles. He raised his hands towards Malcolm: "Look, Malcolm, I don't know what you mean about you being worse than Mack. I don't think you're nastier in the faintest. And anyway, I don't know what goes on inside your head. That's your business."

Malcolm nodded.

Good, he was agreeing, Duffy thought and slipped in, "But I do know you're a good player."

"It's not enough, Duff," Malcolm insisted. "A team needs people who play, yes. But they've got to work for the whole team: top to bottom. I haven't got that. I just haven't got that. The moment the ball's at my feet, it's me, me, me. I know I'm like

170

that." He shook his head sadly.

Duffy knew in himself that he just wasn't following any of this. He took in a breath like he was going deep down underwater: "Then, that's it. I don't get it. I give up. I came over here to see you and start again. But now…" He looked over way beyond the pitches to a tree that was getting ruffled by the wind. He shouted at it, "What's the point?" and his eyes watered up.

Did Malcolm see that? He hoped not. And he hoped Malcolm couldn't hear him so out of breath.

Next thing, he felt Malcolm stand up alongside him and put his hand on his shoulder.

"Hey, man," Malcolm said. "I was just testing you. I said all that stuff just to test you out. All these things with Mack have made me so suspicious. I can't even tell you how suspicious. There

was a moment when I got sucked into Mack's world myself, thinking he was a great guy. Great player – great guy."

Duffy looked up as Malcolm was saying this, swaying to and fro in rhythm to "great player – great guy". It was like that was the way Mack got to you, putting you in a trance like the snake in *The Jungle Book*!

"So I was just seeing if you really did want to come in with us. And you weren't in some kind of secret thing with Mack," Malcolm added.

They touched fists. *That feels good,* Duffy thought.

He brushed his hand across his face like he was wiping the last few minutes away. All this tugging of emotions had got to him. His attention was taken up by someone far off in a tracksuit jogging over to one of the pitches. It was way over the other side where a five-a-side match was on. Duffy watched and Malcolm's eye followed. "Mevlut. He's the medico." Malcolm nodded and it broke the awkwardness between them. "I tell you, they've got everything here. Things are going to be all right, Duff."

Malcolm stepped over to the ball that was nestling under the bench, hoiked it out and tapped it towards Duffy. Duffy flipped it up and kneed it back towards Malcolm. This would have gone on if someone else hadn't turned up – Rossi.

Rossi? Duffy thought. *Wow, had he come over to Angles too?*

Rossi was out of breath. He had been running for some time. By the time he reached Malcolm and Duffy he was panting, shaking his head, and repeating over and over again, "This is bad. This is bad."

"What? What now?" Both Malcolm and Duffy could see that something or other had got worse. But what?

Rossi went on gasping. Duffy wondered if he was putting it on a bit, to cover up something he didn't want to say. He thought Rossi answered him with a "sure!" – but it may have been a gasp.

"What now?" Malcolm asked again.

Rossi went off on "Y'know what I'm saying,

people are saying all sorts of stuff, but then what do you expect? People do that sorta thing and ... and..." Rossi's voice mingled with the breathing again.

Duffy grabbed him by the arm. "Just tell me, Rossi. What's happened?"

Rossi pulled his baseball cap down over his eyes.

This infuriated Duffy now and he yanked it back up.

Rossi looked at both of them. He stopped and fiddled with the cap now, running his fingers along the edge of the peak. "Some guys. I don't know who they were. In Sainsbury's. They attacked Brandon."

Duffy's head went down. This was the worst. He felt Malcolm move towards him and put his hand back on his shoulder. Rossi stood looking from one to the other.

Duffy felt a grim calm come over him. He straightened up: "They wouldn't have done this if I had been there. Mack's done this, though, hasn't he? He's got these other kids to do it for him. We've got to sort this. Malcolm? Rossi? Are we going to do this?"

He wanted more than ever for Malcolm to see that he, Duffy, would stop at nothing now to get rid of Mack, clean out the whole team and start again.

All three put their fists together.

CHAPTER 20

Elgin Radio

*M*ike Le Rose scratched his greying beard and glanced up at the clock. "So to take us up to the hour, here on Elgin Radio, I've got one here for Gordon in … sorry, I can't read the writing here – this is from Brian to you, Gordon, 'Got You On My Mind' with the great Eric Clapton…"

He took a sip from his not-very-hot coffee, and he noticed the stain on the inside of his "Hi from Mike!" Radio Elgin mug. *Shouldn't Jeanette be in by now?* His stubby fingers tapped out a rhythm on the white plastic studio desk where he sat in his swivel chair.

The "Talk to Jeannette" spot followed regularly straight after news, sport and travel on a Thursday afternoon. Or it should.

He pressed the key to get through to studio while Clapton sang on.

"Any sign of Jeannette? What's today's topic, Wrong?"

Ron sat, still, heavy, long-haired but balding, on the other side of the glass: downtrodden Ron, in his aged, fading Glastonbury T-shirt. He had put up with Mike calling him "Wrong" for years. He droned back in his world-on-his-shoulders way, "The seventy-three to Dunsin is not running. She's texted to say we're doing insomnia and other sleep problems."

"Insomnia? That's going to be fun." Mike did his grin-face and faded down Eric Clapton...

"... and after the news, sport and travel, Jeannette is back in the studio – leastways if the seventy-threes are running – hah! – and today we're talking about In. Som. Ni. Ah!" He banged out the syllables, popping his eyes at the same time. "Yes, not being able to sleep and other sleep problems of the night."

His voice switched to his Mr Smooth. "Why can't you sleep? And what do you do to get back to sleep? What other problems do you have in those wee, wee hours? Do you know anyone who sleepwalks? We want to hear from you: text, email or phone. Sorry to have interrupted you, Eric!" And Mike faded the track up again…

No sign of Jeannette during the news. Mike was digging into his memories of not being able to sleep, just in case he would have to fill the gap.

Costas slipped in noiselessly so that listeners wouldn't hear the Elgin Radio studio door bang.

Mike went on musing about sleep, lost sleep, lack of sleep, *Hmm, still no sign of Jeannette*. He realized Costas was already giving out the sports news: "… and here's news of the memorial game coming up, Angles playing Shotfield, in memory of Ash Patel, the inspirational founder of the innovative, youth-led football tournament, something, Mike, that's captured all our hearts, isn't it?"

There was that time before my GCSEs and I kept waking up, Mike mused.

As usual, ignored by Mike, Costas slipped effortlessly into travel: "... a lorry has overturned on the bypass but it's on the verge now, trains all fine, buses all fine apart from the seventy-three. Back to you, Mike."

"Thanks, but no thanks, Costas," Mike laughed. "You know who's on the seventy-three?"

"That guy you bad-mouthed yesterday?" said the ever-keen Costas, with his short, crisp haircut framing his face, leaning into the microphone.

Ah, Costas, Mike pondered. Dear Costas, ever hopeful that one day some big-time radio station manager would be listening to him from his Porsche

and would call Costas up to come and work for his big-time radio station instead of doing sport and travel on little old Elgin.

"Bad-mouthed? Me? Never! Nice try, Costas," said Mike, "No! I meant Jeannette. Our Jeannette is stuck on the little old seventy-three. We're supposed to be doing insomnia!" He knew he was filling the time.

"Insomnia?" Costas understood the game going on here. "I'm the world expert on insomnia, Mike. Last time that I had a night's sleep was ... let me ... see, Maria is five, George is three and now little Tony. Yes, five years ago."

Mike laughed again. "That's not insomnia, Costas. That's babies. Insomnia – big word. Babies – little word. I do the big words, you do the little ones."

The door opened and Jeannette walked in, wearing a brand-new dark blue dress, her make-up in a perfect state, her notebook already open and a silver ballpoint neatly slotted in its place down the side.

"Hey, folks," Mike said, taking off his earphones

and waving to her, "seems like at least one of those delayed seventy-threes got through because Jeannette has just breezed in."

"Great to see you, Jeannette," Costas called out, hoping that Ron had kept his microphone open.

Mike waved him out of the studio with an irritated hand. "Time for some afternoon shut-eye, Costas. You've got another sleepless night coming up, remember. Isn't it your turn to do the nappy-change tonight?"

Costas got the point. His time was up. And Mike had neatly made him look less like a smooth broadcaster and more like any old stressed dad. Costas strode out of the studio, not as quietly as he had come in, pushing the heavy, soundproof door with an angry shove.

"Yes, folks," Mike picked up the thread, "we are talking about those long nights, those long, long nights when cares and troubles come into your mind and you can't sleep. Or perhaps you have other kinds of sleep problems. Text, email or phone. Jeannette, lovely to see you, welcome back to our

'Talk with Jeannette' moment." Mike put on his I'm-really-interested face.

"Thanks, Mike. Good afternoon all, and especially those of you for whom this is an extremely serious matter." Jeannette threw a glance towards Mike. She had picked up a hint that perhaps he wasn't going to take today's topic as seriously as he should, or as seriously as she would like.

"Serious?" Mike stared up at one of the dull light bulbs deeply embedded into the dark grey ceiling.

"Well, Mike, night is the time when thoughts we keep hidden during the day come to us. They might keep us awake, or indeed affect us in ways that we don't fully understand."

Jeannette was indeed taking this very seriously. Serious was today's note. Mike pulled himself together, switched off his joke brain. "Interesting you say that, Jeannette," Mike said. "I've got a text here from a Mrs MB. She says, 'The other day, I woke up very early, and I realized that in the night I must have got up and written on a bit of paper that was on the table and then put it in an envelope. Is that possible?' Jeannette?"

"Mrs MB, if you're listening," Jeannette said quietly and carefully, "it is possible. Yes, it is."

Mike interrupted, "And if you are listening, Mrs MB, call us. We'd love to talk to you. So, Jeannette, sleepwalking. What's that all about?

"Well, in a word, Mike, we don't really know. We can describe it, but…"

As Jeannette went on, Ron waved from the other side of the window. It was the first movement he had made all day. Mike realized that he hadn't put his earphones back on and quickly pushed them over the top of his head.

"She's on three," Ron droned.

Mike did a thumbs-up and waved Jeannette to carry on.

"… but … we don't really know why one person walks in their sleep and another person has very disturbed dreams and might roll about in the bed but then doesn't actually walk."

"Thank you, yes," Mike said, almost butting

in, "and I think we have Mrs MB on the line now, thank you so much for calling in. This must be very distressing for you."

But there was silence. Mike waited. Jeannette waited. Mike looked through the window to Ron with a questioning look on his face. Ron did nothing.

They could hear that someone was there. But there was nothing. No words. Suddenly the studio felt cold. Mike waited for Jeannette to say something. Jeannette waited for Mike. The faint, far off breathing went on. *Was there really someone there?*

Finally, Jeannette said very quietly, "Yes? Mrs MB?"

And a woman's voice came back, "I can't stop myself. I can't stop myself." And the voice stopped again.

Jeannette and Mike waited again.

"Last night, I ... I ... woke up and I was standing over the sink. I was washing my son's football kit. Over and over again. I couldn't get it clean. I couldn't wash it clean. I was washing and washing…"

Mrs MB's voice was taking on a strange rhythm.

"...whatever I used to wash the kit with, I couldn't get it clean. I couldn't get it clean."

Mike opened his hand towards Jeannette, cueing her up to make a comment. Jeannette put her hand to her front to say that she was listening and sympathizing with what Mrs MB was saying.

"Now, I don't know if I was awake or asleep or if I dreamed it or not. I don't know how I got to the sink to wash the kit. I don't know any of it. I don't know any of it. For a moment I thought I was washing the kit that belonged to other boys ... Banksy's kit..."

For some reason, in that instant, the studio lights dimmed. Mike and Jeannette looked up sharply, and they both looked through to Ron. Ron sat as still as ever, unmoved.

Mrs MB didn't stop. "What's done is done. What's done can't be undone, can it?"

Still, Jeannette didn't say anything. Mike waited. He felt he had intruded on something he would rather not have heard. What was this all about? This was, he thought, a very, very disturbed woman.

"And then I went back to bed. I went back to bed."

That seemed to be the end of it.

Jeannette sensed as much and said, "Mrs MB, thank you so much for calling in to talk to me, can I ask you a question?"

There was no answer.

"Mrs MB?"

Again no answer. It was as if it hadn't been a person. Just a voice. And the voice had passed through the studio. It had come in, hung there for a few seconds, said its piece and moved on out, like a whisper on the wind.

Mike looked at Jeannette. Her face, usually so composed, was rumpled and disturbed. She was frowning and Mike thought she must have rubbed

her eye while Mrs MB had been talking because a small smudge of mascara marked her cheek.

"A difficult moment, there," Mike said, trying to pull it all back to reality. "I tell you what, let's have another track and we'll be back straight after with more of your thoughts about sleepless nights. Here's Sting, with 'I Can't Stop Thinking About You'."

The track started. Mike leaned forward and caught Jeannette's eye. "You OK?"

She shrugged.

Mike shrugged back.

And they were both left with their thoughts about what had actually happened in that minute Mrs MB had been on the line.

CHAPTER 21

Lennox

"So it's come to this. On or off the pitch." Lennox was pacing up and down, muttering, trying to get his mind clear by saying things to himself, his breath steaming around his face. "It's good: Angles versus Shotfield. The only way to sort it."

He could see it clearly: Mack had wormed his way up to the top and was ruining the whole of this Youth League thing. This was the chance to get it sorted. Once and for all.

"What?"

Lennox jolted. *Who said that?*

It was Mento, who had arrived on the edge of the field with his mates, Kai and Angus. *Wow,* Lennox thought, *Mento – that's another one of the guys from Shotfield who has come over to Angles. Kai and Angus included.* "Oh, you know, just thinking."

The tower blocks at the side of the canal nearby loomed up, silent witnesses to what was about to happen in this big game. This was going to be huge.

"What's happening?" Lennox said to them.

"Looking good, man." Mento nodded. "You know Malcolm's playing?"

"Sure," Lennox said, feeling all the better for hearing Malcolm's name.

"And Siefert."

"Right." Lennox was putting these guys that Mento was reeling off into their positions, like a round of Fantasy Football playing in his mind.

"Duffy, of course."

Mento seemed to have it all in his head. Lennox smiled to himself.

Kai butted in. "What about Donal and his brother ... whatshisname?"

"No, I don't think so." Lennox pulled out his phone and looked at some texts that had come in. "No, but I got a text that Siefert's bro is playing, and some names here I don't know..."

Mento stepped closer. "You got any news on the other side, on ... y'know?"

Lennox knew that Mento didn't need to say Mack's name. In fact, Lennox mused, it was almost as if they both knew it would be unlucky to say it out loud. The dull, cold sky seemed to be pressing down on them.

Kai joined in. "I heard that he's going nuts."

"Yeah, well," Angus added, as if he was saying something important.

Lennox looked at him and realized Angus had

said nothing.

"Y'know what I mean," Angus added, "I mean … I mean he knows he's losing it. He's bossing people about, and they only do what he says 'cos he's the big-I-am, not 'cos they think he's great or anything."

"Yeah." Lennox nodded. "He'll probably end up renaming Shotfield. He'll call it Macbeth United!"

Angus snorted grimly.

"He's not fit to wear the shirt," Angus added, more to himself than to the others, and Lennox watched him try to blow his breath-cloud away.

Mento looked towards the tower blocks. "I reckon it's all getting to him. He must know what he's done."

Kai stretched his arms wide and then up, then down, and did a quarter squat and held it there. "C'mon, guys, keep warmed up. I pulled my calf the other week 'cos I didn't do my stretches on that really cold day."

The others joined in. Kai took

that as a cue to be the little leader for that small moment. "We can get it back to how it was, eh?" He looked round at the others.

Lennox felt the good vibe coming from Kai. *Yes,* he thought. This was feeling like cleaning out a locker in the changing-room, like when some old wet shorts left in there had started to stink and they were making everything else in there start to whiff too. He pumped his fist forwards. "We can do this!" he said with an urgent edge in his voice.

CHAPTER 22

Macbeth

*M*acbeth sat on the bus headed to the training ground, looking out of the window at some people shoving each other outside McDonalds. His phone went. He glanced down to see who it was: *Huh! That jerk Savva,* he thought. *If you don't feel down before you hear from him, you always do when you listen to him.*

"Yeah?" Macbeth said in as unenthusiastic a way as he could manage.

Sure enough, Savva was going on about what a

great team Angles were putting out.

Macbeth tried not to listen to him. Into his mind came that weird time he was in that room and those scouts were talking about what might or might not happen: how he was OK so long as they didn't move their training base. Check. And the only kind of kid who could threaten him was someone who didn't have a name. As if. Like, who hasn't got a name? Oh no, Savva was still going on and on.

"They've got some good players, Mack," he whined.

"They're mice!" Macbeth snapped back.

"No, no, I mean—"

Finally, Macbeth had had enough. "Look, just shut it, will you? What's the matter with you? You're such a wuss. It's all over your face. When the others look at you, I can see it: they feel like giving up."

But Savva wouldn't let it go. "No, Mack, Angles are really good, they're—"

Macbeth hit the *home* key. That got rid of him.

Macbeth looked out of the window again.

Ahead was the Avenue, a dreary stretch of road that had, ever since he was very young, seemed so lonely. Lonely Lane, he used to call it. And now, looking at it, he felt that loneliness. He imagined what it would be like to be with a real close mate at this moment, instead of trying to do it all on his own.

A text came up on his phone:

Angles here already.

So what? So darned what? *Why's everyone trying to needle me?* he thought. *Even that kid Seifert, who I thought was with me. And anyway, where's Mum? Is she going to be at the game or not? She had said something about having had a bad night. Yeah, yeah.*

Lonely Lane was still doing its lonely work on his mind.

He called home.

A silky voice answered. It was a woman, but it wasn't Mum. "Hello?"

"Hello?" Macbeth parroted. "You're not Mum."

The voice took that as a question. "She's not

well. I'm talking to her."

Who is this? Was it one of those people Mum means when she says she's going to "see" someone about some problems she has?

Mack thought some more, and the voice echoed in his mind ... like he had heard it before. *Where, though? One of the teachers? Or on the radio, was it?*

"Your mother is in a bad place," the voice went on. "She's having visions."

"Well, that'll be because she hasn't taken her pills. Even I know that."

"It's not as simple as that." The voice had some steel in it now.

"Well, don't bother me with it!" Mack replied sharply. "See yer," and again he hit the *home* button to cut her off.

Yes, it was definitely one of Mum's weirdo people she liked to "see".

As the bus passed the chemists, a picture came into his mind again of Mum's bedside drawer and the little boxes, and jars and bottles of pills, potions,

creams and ointments she kept in there. *What IS the matter with her?* he thought. All that stuff, and none of it does any good, I bet. He went on looking into the open drawer as it sat there in his mind. *Imagine if you could take some of that stuff and it could sort out everything! I don't know what kind of team I've got today. The best guys have gone over to Angles, anyway. If we lose, I'm done for, aren't I?* His mind felt like it was racing downhill and nothing could stop it. But then, again, the memory of those weird scout guys came to him. *You'll be OK so long as the training base isn't moved.*

A text came up on the phone. It was from home.

She's not coming.

Mack texted back:

I know.

And then the reply:

I can keep you posted with how she is.

Mack frowned. And threw a thought at the phone without turning it into a text:

I don't care. I don't even know you. I don't want to know you. Go away, weird person.

CHAPTER 23

Malcolm

*L*ennox and the rest were well into the last stages of their warm-up, deep stretches towards the muddy grass, when Malcolm arrived with Duffy, Rossi, Seifert, Seifert's mate and some others, their boots padding on the ground.

Malcolm felt a strong surge of a good feeling to see everyone. Good to see that they had all remembered their kit. *Even the socks.* Great.

It was all high fives and slaps for a bit, when his phone buzzed in his tracksuit pocket. He pulled himself away from the others to take a look at it. It was a text:

Training Pitch 9.

Training Pitch 9? he thought... *But weren't we supposed to be on that other pitch?*

He looked out and across the grass and back to his phone.

The tower blocks watched over them as they waited.

CHAPTER 24

Macbeth

*M*acbeth went to swing off the bus as he usually did, but his foot got caught on the metal rim of the step and he stumbled on to the pavement, his bag hitting him as he tottered.

He straightened himself out and started walking towards the ground. He pulled his phone out to check on whether he had a full team or not.

One of the guys had texted that he was still having his breakfast.

Breakfast?! He felt himself explode inside. *You're going on about breakfast and we're just about to face the game of our lives. This is a make-or-break thing for me. I don't suppose you care.* Macbeth was just about to text him to drop his breakfast, right now, starve if necessary, and get over to the game, when another text came through from home. *Oh, why doesn't she leave it?* he thought. *I so don't need to be thinking about that stuff.*

`She's gone to bed. I have sedated her.`

Sedated? Sedated? As he ploughed on towards the ground, he really didn't need to be thinking about what "sedated" was about. *What does it even mean?* He racked his mind for a memory of the word. *Oh yes,* he remembered Mum saying it about one time she had some kind of black-out or something and the doctor had given her ... his mind wandered back to the drawer full of pills. Something to do with sending you to sleep. And then he remembered that bother Mum had had about sleep. In that moment, it was almost as if he could taste the bitterness of pills when you can't swallow them, and they stick on your tongue and start to dissolve.

A car revved beside him, moved on and round the corner ahead, till it was gone. The word "dissolve" walked round Macbeth's mind for a moment, and he remembered a chemistry lesson at school when they put some stuff – *what was it?* – at the bottom of a glass beaker and it slowly disappeared. *That's what happens,* he thought. *You do something today and then it just dissolves.* Like the sound his steps were making on the pavement. *That step! One moment it's a sound and the next it's gone.*

He texted back to whoever it was:

`Praps yu shld have done that b4.`

As he was texting, Messem, one of the guys who was definitely playing today, was running towards him – away from the ground. *Oh no,* Macbeth thought, *he's not dropping out, is he? Got a broken eyelash, has he?*

"Mack! Mack!" Messem was shouting.

"What?" Macbeth said, "What are you doing, man? You're going the wrong way."

"No, that's what I'm trying to say, Mack."

Mack felt anger rising in his throat. "What are you trying to say?" He was shouting.

Messem spat it out. "It's been moved or something. It's not at the training ground you said. Like I'm trying to tell you. It's … er … pitch nine."

Macbeth felt himself caught in a cold grip. The days and nights between now and that time when he met the scouts collapsed and he heard the echoey sound of them talking about the training ground being moved. There was a rush in his mind about how ridiculous he had thought it was that the training ground could move, but here and right now, yes, right now, the training ground was being moved. They wouldn't be playing where they had all agreed they would play.

"Pitch nine?" he spat it out and right back at Messem, like it was his fault.

Messem nodded, looking amazed that Macbeth would have got that worked up about it.

"If you're lying, Mess, if this is some kind of trick, you're going to get it."

"No, I'm not... Look, it's not that big a deal, is it?"

Macbeth wasn't going to answer that. He stumbled on towards the field. *No,* he thought, *it's not that big a deal unless you're me.* He looked up at the sky. *Old, cold, grey sky. How could you get so fed up that even the sky was fed up?*

He looked at the tower blocks as they got nearer and nearer.

And you lot can clear off, Macbeth thought at them, as they grew in front of his eyes.

CHAPTER 25

Malcolm

a crow flapped its way over pitch nine. It looked down at the grass below, hoping to see some bit of fried chicken, or bit of sandwich crushed into the mud, but all it saw was two clusters at either end of the pitch: the one loose and careless, with players looking out and away from the cluster, kicking their feet into the mud; the other, tight, together and looking in, pressing their minds to what was to come. The crow flapped down to a crossbar to watch.

Malcolm was talking, his voice tense and breathy. "OK, guys, we've got this. Seifert, I want you up front, today. Duff, you're centre-mid. Keep the ball moving."

Seifert barked back, "We can do this. No more Mack!"

Duffy looked down at the new kit. The youth management had added an embroidered ash-tree leaf to the Angles badge as a tribute to Ash Patel, the founder of the regional youth-led tournament and who had, sadly, passed away a few weeks earlier. He touched it. When the others saw him do that, they touched their leaves too.

Malcolm put his cold
fist to his mouth and blew
into it to warm it up, but
surprised himself at the low
whistle that came out. *It's an
echo of the whistle that's going to start the game,*
he thought.

"Bring it on!" he shouted.

And the rest of the team roared back as they
moved out on to the pitch to take up their positions.

The crow took off from the crossbar, looking
again to see if this time, there was something for
him to drop on to and tear apart.

CHAPTER 26

Macbeth

*I*t's *not about playing well, Mack,* he remembered his mother saying, *it's about winning. Nothing else matters.*

Her words drilled into his ear: "No matter what those snowflake coaches tell you, that's the truth, that's what counts in life. The only thing anyone cares about is whether you bring that trophy home."

He had taken up a position, "in the pocket", a slot behind the striker, in front of centre-mid where he could keep an eye on everything, move back into a more defensive position if need be, or further forward to score. *This has to be about me. If I win this, the ones who've sneaked off to Angles will come back to me, and then – hah! – see the coaches and the scouts hanging round me then! I can do this. The only thing in my way now is that stuff the weird guys in the room said about meeting some little Johnny No-name!* He laughed inside.

A freezing wind wrapped itself around his legs. He glanced towards the touchline, as he always did, half-expecting to see Mum, in place where she had been in every game he had ever played before. And then he remembered the lonely sound of the woman saying that she was "sedated"... So cool, so

hospital-like.

Almost without noticing it, the game had begun. Angles were getting a good bit of possession, flicking the ball about at the back, trying to pull Shotfield out of position. He waved them back. "Shape, Shots!" he yelled at them.

He sensed that his guys weren't getting stuck in. They weren't going in for the tackles, and Angles were starting to probe. Mento and Kai did a neat one-two, but he anticipated it. *They think I'm beaten but I know more about this game than all of them together,* he thought. But he kept his head down. He didn't want to look into the eyes of the guys who used to play for Shotfield: Len, Duff, Angus and the rest.

Just then, Seifert was coming towards him. He had the ball well under control, slipping it from left to right and back to left. He could always use both feet, Macbeth remembered. But as Seifert took it one more time on to his right, Macbeth held his ground. Then, as Seifert played the ball round Macbeth, Seifert muttered, "Plonker!" at him and pushed the ball on.

At that, Macbeth felt the old rage rise in his throat. He rammed his foot right across and into Seifert's legs just as he was about to follow the ball he had so neatly pushed ahead. Seifert's standing leg buckled and crunched into the other leg. He screamed and fell to the ground. In a flash,

everyone could see that Seifert was out of the game.

Not so much Johnny No-name, Macbeth thought, *more like Johnny No-game. Don't call me Plonker and think you can get away with it.*

These thoughts didn't last long because, in the break of play, Duffy raced towards Macbeth and squared up to him. It was going to get nasty. The other Angles rushed round and pulled Duffy back, telling him one hand on Mack and he'd be off. They could get a sub on for Seifert and win this. With Duffy on a red, it would be difficult.

Duffy nodded. He knew his mates were right, but he stared at Macbeth, as if hoping to kill him with a look. Macbeth kept his head down. The look got lost in the wind.

The game started up again and Macbeth was desperate to gain the initiative. He urged his players forward, shouting, "We can do them on pace! I know this lot, they haven't got it in their legs!"

He was pleased to see that at least two or three of the team responded. A neat move down the right, on the overlap. A cut-in. He threw himself forward and yelled, "Cross it first time, cross it!" But the player paused, turned and made to pass it back. Mack threw his hands in the air.

It distracted Duffy, who was closing in on the Shotfield player, and there was space for a break.

"Now!" Macbeth yelled, and the ball came towards him. If he could pivot on his left foot, he'd get a shot on goal. He waited and then darted towards the ball to give him space. In a split second's time, he would get in his shot – *bottom right, bottom right*, flashed into his mind.

But as he pulled back his foot, he felt a shove. Malcolm did that old trick of going for the ball but somehow or another getting the opposition player out of the way at the same time. Macbeth tumbled, and as he did he clawed at Malcolm's leg, yelling,

"Ref! Ref!"

But the ref was unmoved. Looked clean to him.

Malcolm had possession and smooth as you like slipped the ball to Duffy, who fed the ball forward and out to Kai. Malcolm raced forward and Kai played the ball beautifully into the corridor of uncertainty for Malcolm to rush on to and score.

Macbeth, still lying on the ground, pounded the grass with his fists in frustration.

CHAPTER 27

Macbeth

*O*ne-nil. Big deal, Macbeth snorted to himself. He thought of the great comebacks he had watched on TV. *Two-nil down – even three-nil, and wasn't it Liverpool who came back and won it? I'm not going to chuck it in, am I?*

He dropped back towards the goal. The keeper was about to slug it upfield. Macbeth waved angrily at him to roll it out to the fullback. The keeper shrugged, knowing that it would invite the Angles forwards to close him down. High-pressing always caused them trouble, even when they were at full strength. The fullback took it, and two Angles players closed in on him. Again, Macbeth waved angrily. In that wave was all the anger, hate and ambition that he had been through in the last few weeks.

The fullback managed to slip the ball between the advancing Angles players. Macbeth heard Duffy behind him gasp in disappointment. The ball came neatly to Macbeth's feet and he swivelled, still keeping close possession. As he did so, he felt Duffy was on to him, just a short space away.

It was a decisive moment in the game. Angles' positioning was all over the place. By high-pressing they were short at the back, and out of shape. All Macbeth had to do was either dribble past Duffy or slip a pass through to his striker and they were in on goal. Macbeth could see it all in a split second. *That's why I am so darned good,* he thought.

Duffy closed on him. *Dribble or pass?* A dribble and he could leave him for dead. And he, Macbeth, would be the hero. He could take it on upfield, forget the striker and even the score. *Dribble it is!* And he dummied a tap to the left, slipped his foot over the ball and pulled it back to the right. *Skills! Tekkers!*

But Duffy was somehow bigger (or was it quicker?) than Macbeth was expecting and he was on to him, using his upper-body strength to push Macbeth back. Macbeth resisted. *I've got it there as well*, he thought.

"Who do you think you are?" Macbeth muttered as he held the ball away from Duffy, "Johnny No-name?"

Out of the corner of his eye, Macbeth could see that this delay was giving Angles time to drop back and get their shape again. He had to keep possession and, if necessary, do a back pass.

In the pause, he heard Duffy laugh and grunt, "Funny you should say that: yeah!"

Macbeth sensed the Angles players coming in towards them to close down the out-ball. He was in trouble here. *Maybe a back-heel, if only that jerk of a fullback would come in tight to help out.*

Duffy wasn't leaving that Johnny No-Name thing. "Middle name's Nott. My mum's family name. Geddit, plonker?"

Macbeth back-heeled it anyway, fullback up for the ball or not. As he said "*not*" to himself, he heard himself think "*Nott-Duffy*". *Not Duffy*. He felt the breath go from his chest.

The fullback was nowhere near the back pass, Duffy was on to it, did a superb one-two with Malcolm and curved the ball into the far corner.

The cool, sharp way he did it told Macbeth that the game was up. There would be no way back from this. Angles were better in attack and defence. They had transitioned beautifully. They had several players who were playing box to box. *And my lot?* Macbeth looked at them. *They aren't playing for me. They're a bunch of can't-play, won't-play losers. And what does that make me?*

As the sky darkened, the mud got thicker, and the seconds dragged out into never-ending minutes.

The breath that had left him earlier didn't come back. Now in his chest there was a nothing. Instead of his legs carrying him forward, he felt as if he was dragging his legs. All that hope and ambition, the dreams of what could happen and should happen, were getting swallowed up in the dark, wet earth at his feet.

Above, he heard a crow laughing at him.

CHAPTER 28

Malcolm

*I*t was a bitter changing room after the game. The sweaty air was full of contempt and hate. Macbeth sat struggling with one of his boots.

Malcolm stood over him, watching what Mack was trying to do: the lace on his boot seemed to have iced into the mud, and by the look of it, his hands were too cold to get in and work it loose. Malcolm could see that his arms looked weak and his eyes, either wet from the cold or from shame, were making it hard for him to see what his fingers were trying to do.

Malcolm stepped nearer into Mack's body-space. "You don't deserve to be here, Mack... You don't deserve to be a coach or a captain or even to play this game. I should have seen it earlier. You're a liar, a cheat and a snake. You very nearly ruined it for all of us."

Malcolm watched as Mack tried to make an effort to protest, to defend himself. "I ... I..." but nothing came out.

And Malcolm watched as the struggle to get the lace loose went on and on and on without end.

"This whole league could have fallen apart because of you and what you've tried to do. But you haven't got away with it."

Malcolm knew he had to finish this thing off, to go in for the kill. He turned away from Mack as Mack's fingers froze even more on the mud on his boot.

"Guys!" Malcolm called out as he raised his arm in the air.

And all he needed to do was beckon and every single one of the players – Angles and all the weary, fed-up Shotfield players too – grabbed their kit, the odd shirt, ball, shinpad, no matter whether they were fully changed or not, and followed Malcolm out of the changing-room door.

Mack was left on his own, the cold, hard boot still firmly stuck on his foot.

CHAPTER 29

Elgin Radio

*M*ike Le Rose was scoffing raisins out of his hand to keep his energy levels up. He swivelled round in his chair to look out at the car park, while the Rolling Stones' "It's All Over Now" played out...

He faded it down over the last guitar solo. "And believe it or not, folks, while Sir Mick was keeping us going there, I have just looked out over the great Elgin Radio car park and seen – hold your breath – a break in the clouds. Costas is here with weather, sport and some hard-luck story, I shouldn't be surprised. Costas, is it a break in the clouds, or am I seeing things?"

Costas was delighted to be back on-air and was quick to say, "Well, Mike, we can never put it past you to be seeing things, but yes, it was what's technically known as 'blue sky' and—"

Mike chipped back, "It's OK, Costas, we won't be expecting anything so grand as any blue-sky thinking from you. What's with the sport?"

Costas tried not to sound disappointed that Mike had got the sneery better of him yet again, so carried on regardless: "I'll be doing the national sport on the hour, Mike, but local sport now and news in from the local youth league: it seems as if there's been a big change-around here. Shotfield, the club that was doing so well recently, has folded."

Mike was halfway interested. "Really? That IS a turn-around for the books," he said, never afraid to use a cliché when his brain wasn't fully in gear.

"Yup," said Costas, "seems they've folded. Not sure why. But there's an upside to this: Angles have taken over the whole tournament. They're going to divide things up, A, B, C and D teams, run a mini-league, organize the cup, the whole shebang. If only their founder Ash Patel were here today to see it."

"Who's shebang?" said Mike, doing his stupid shtick.

Costas was on to it. "C'mon, Mike. You know. Shebang: played for Bayern Munich in the 1990s."

"Thanks, Costas, leave your joke in the bin on the way out. And now I have a request in for Pharrell and 'Happy'. Anyone not joining in with the lovely Pharrell Williams will find that the Mike Le Rose Happy Gang will be down your way to see that you do. Here we go, Pharrell, tell us what happy is, man!"

Mike sat back in his chair and looked up at the lights in the ceiling.

For some reason that he couldn't quite put his finger on, life felt good, and he hoped that other people were feeling that way too.

Michael Rosen

Michael is one of the best-known figures in the children's book world, renowned for his work as a poet, performer, broadcaster, professor, scriptwriter and author of classic books such as *We're Going on a Bear Hunt*. He was Children's Laureate from 2007–2009.

Tony Ross

After training at Liverpool School of Art, Tony worked as a cartoonist, graphic designer, advertising art director and art lecturer. Today he is best known for the *Horrid Henry* and *Little Princess* series of books, as well as illustrating books for David Walliams.

About William Shakespeare

William Shakespeare is regarded as the greatest English playwright in history.

Born in Warwickshire in 1564, his work consists of 39 plays, and over 150 sonnets. His plays have been translated into every living language in the world! Some of Shakespeare's most famous works include Romeo and Juliet, Hamlet, King Lear and Othello.

Macbeth is thought to have been first performed in 1606. It is one of the plays that he wrote during the reign of King James I, who was the patron of Shakespeare's acting company. It is thought that like many plays Shakespeare wrote, Macbeth clearly shows Shakespeare's own attitudes to what dangers lie in being the wrong kind of king or ruler.

Shakespeare wrote the play to show the damaging

effects on a person or a whole society of political ambition. It tells the story of a brave but violent Scottish general who receives a prophecy that he will one day become king. Consumed by ambition, and encouraged by his wife, Macbeth murders King Duncan, takes the throne for himself and then takes desperate measures to stay in power.

Macbeth has inspired many films, plays and adaptations over the years. It remains a vivid reminder of the physical, psychological and social impact of seeking power for your own gain.

Join Michael Rosen and Tony Ross with their unforgettable retelling of Charles Dickens's beloved classic. Harry Gruber plays the role of Scrooge in his school's production of *A Christmas Carol,* and he is extra nervous about tonight's performance because his father is in the audience – not away for business, as usual. Will the story's message of Christmas cheer and the redemptive power of love reach his father's distracted heart?

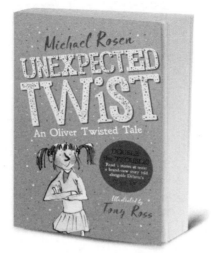

An original story by Michael Rosen, inspired by the Charles Dickens classic *Oliver Twist*. Shona and her dad are moving house, and at Shona's new school, the rules are pretty confusing; she keeps getting into trouble without realizing! After Shona is unexpectedly given a mobile phone, she begins to suspect there's something fishy about the new boys she's met. Some gifts, she comes to learn, aren't exactly free. Another Dickens classic reimagined by the dream team of Michael Rosen and Tony Ross.